After the World Ended
Hannah Lackoff

AFTER THE WORLD ENDED
An 18thWall Productions book published by
arrangement with Hannah Lackoff
verba mea in manibus
desiderium meum .
Text Copyright © Hannah Lackoff
Cover illustration by Jason Bhenke
Design by Elisgraphics

See page 242 for previous publications and permissions.

To my parents, my first publishers,
For writing down my early stories and stapling them into books

Thank you to my family for being the readers and scribes of my very first stories. Thank you to teachers and classmates at Medomak Valley and Wheaton College where many of these stories began, and especially to Anna who helped me to fill many red notebooks and word processor files with writing games and teenage novellas. Thanks to James and everyone at 18thWall for first believing in "The Mirror," and then the whole world-ending package. And thank you to George, for planning a wedding with me while I worked on this book, and for everything else.

Table of Contents

After the World Ended

We didn't know anyone was left, after the world ended. We assumed we were the only survivors, which was sad, but not really for us because we were still alive. We shrugged our shoulders and went on with the planting and sowing and reaping and hoeing and the fishing, hunting, gathering, and mending. It had always been quiet on our little spit peninsula, and now it was just a little bit quieter.

On the day Timor arrived, Pap was up on the hill with the goats. We had to baby them a little more now; now that they might be the only goats left in existence. We used to boss them around and smack them with sticks, but now we just kind of followed them all over the hills until they were ready to go back home. We picked up their poop too, which had felt a little weird at first, but there was really nothing like it for fertilizer and if our crops didn't grow it wasn't like we could drive to the store and pick up replacements.

Pap came running down the hill and the goats came running after him, and they were all yelling so loud we couldn't distinguish between them.

"There's a man!" called Pap when he got closer, "A man! Be careful Leslie, he might want to breed with our women!"

We laughed for a good while, but it turns out he wasn't joking. There really was a man coming, though his intentions with our women were unclear. We all walked to the top of the hill with the goats and Rosie, and the sun was setting behind us over the water and I'm sure it was all a very dramatic introduction.

Timor, though we didn't know that was his name, was tall and dark and shiny against the pale grass. His clothes were a little worn, but he was definitely alive despite the fact that the world had ended. When he got close enough we started to wave and jump up and down, and Pap shouted "Halloo!" and we thought we might have heard a faint "Halloo!" back, but we couldn't be sure. Then Rosie started barking her least threatening of all her non-threatening barks and bounded down the hill in a blur of brown fuzz until she got to the stranger, whereupon she threw herself down at his feet and waited for a belly rub.

He bent down a little tiredly and pushed his hands and face into her fuzzy side. Then he stood up, and she stood up, and she took hold of his sleeve in her mouth and led him up the hill to where we were standing.

"Hello," said Pap guardedly.

"Hello," said the stranger. They stood for few moments in an old-west style standoff; two men heading up two different fragments of the world.

"I thought you was dead." said Pap finally.

"Me?" said the stranger.

"We thought everybody was dead!" squeaked Pippa.

"Well," said the stranger ponderously, "I'm not."

Mam and Pap nodded in satisfaction. They liked neatness and concise answers. This man could fit into their worldview a-okay.

"Come on back to the homestead," said Pap, "we'll show you around." Since the end of the world, Pap's language had converted to that of an earlier time. He said *was dead* instead of *were dead*, *homestead* instead of *house*. At any effort of Mam's corrections he would patiently explain that there was nobody left except her who cared what he talked like.

"I expected guns, not generosity," said the stranger.

"Guns?" asked Pap, "You think we'd waste our bullets on a human?"

"Not many visitors in these parts, eh?" He was smiling a little, but

8

he still looked tired.

"You're the first!" Pap said it proudly; he was practically beaming.

"Must be mighty quiet up here," the new man said, and that shut us all up so we could show him the color of our silence; how it was full of crickets and cicadas and the hum of the river and the ripple of grass. He stood up on the hill and breathed in real soft and kind of held the sound inside him for a moment.

"That's nice," he said, breathing out the apples growing and Rosie scratching and the goats all chewing on whatever they could find. "The world gets so loud sometimes, you know?" And we all nodded and murmured our assent, as though we hadn't been living with nothing but that quiet color for the past seventeen months. I was almost sixteen and I could barely remember what the world sounded like before. This stranger's voice rocked me to the core with its new vibrations.

"Canter," said my father, "You and Jessup go on ahead and get everything ready.

"Get what ready, Pap?" asked Jessup. She was fourteen.

"Everything, you know, everything!" Pap waived his hands impatiently and we took off running towards home, shouting at the silence. We were pioneer women, we were brave explorers and musicians and construction workers!

"You know why we had to go home first, don't you Jess?" I asked.

"Why?" she said, because she wanted me to say it, even though she already knew.

"Because we're of breeding age!" I shouted. "We're ripe for baby making and we have no one to share it with!"

She giggled and giggled and I poked her in the belly, even though, of course, baby making was all theoretical since there was no one but our older brother who we even could have made babies with, not since the world had come to a grinding halt everywhere except here.

We didn't know what Pap wanted, so we swept the kitchen floor and hid all the dirty dishes and got out a buffet of our most plentiful food; soda bread and cider and corn grits with bacon fat. We weren't sure if Pap had meant for us to dress up so the stranger would want to breed with us or dress down so he wouldn't, so we stayed in our faded jeans and dusty t-shirts. We were breathless with nerves and couldn't say why.

Pap and Mam came in with the stranger, who they said was named Timor. He looked more worn out than we did from up close. He ate a slice of soda bread with fat spread on it, drank three glasses of cider, and fell asleep with his head on the table.

Pippa poked the end of his nose, which was very red and swollen like something had stung it.

"Where'd he come from?" she said in a loud whisper. Mam shoed her away and told everyone to get back to what they were doing, but Pap sat down across from Timor and just watched him. I went out to find out where the goats had landed.

They were at the bottom of the hill, eating some wild mushrooms and looking very pleased with themselves.

I kicked the tops of the grass at them but they ignored me. I poked Butterbean in the rump and shook Kale's horns, but they just blinked their vertical eyes at me and chewed some more. The sun started to set and I got fed up with being nice to goats, of all things, so I clapped my hands and waved my arms and shouted "Home! Home!" just like we used too, and they remembered everything and I ran behind them back to their pen. I shut the gate and gave them some water and they bleated grumpily at me.

I took off my shoes when I went inside, both to save the soles and to keep the house cleaner. Timor was still snoring at the table, but Jessup had taken Pap's place across from him.

"Would you want to have babies with him?" She was scrutinizing his dusty skin and his stubbly hair, his slightly different clothes and the way his breathing sounded.

"I don't want to have babies with anyone."

"You might have to though. Like if we have to repopulate the planet."

"I guess so." I said, even though I didn't.

"I think he's handsome. I like his little spots." Timor had dark freckles on his nose and cheeks, which wrinkled when he smiled, and he was awake. Jessup gasped and turned pink and ran out of the room. Timor looked at me.

"What about you?" he said, and his voice was velvety like cider. "Do you like my spots?"

I didn't want to answer so I told him, "She's embarrassed." Then I felt embarrassed too, like maybe I was being rude, so I told him, "Your spots are fine by me."

"You girls are so refreshing," he said, and Pap heard him laughing and came back in.

We went to sleep that night and dreamed of the stranger, of Timor, of the possibility of a world outside our own. And when we awoke, he was not a dream, but sleeping on our couch under the spare quilt, snoring softly.

Aaron came in from the water with some fresh-caught fish which we cooked up for breakfast. The electricity had stopped working suddenly months ago so we cooked everything on the wood stove. When summer came we were planning on building a pit outside so the

11

house wouldn't get too hot. For now, though, it was cozy on a crisp spring morning, and the smell of fish frying was mouth-watering and homey.

Timor ate his portion faster than anyone else, and he sucked on the bones and squished the eyeballs between his teeth without anyone having to tell him how wasteful it would be if he left them behind.

"What's it like out there?" asked Pap.

Timor shook his head slowly, looked down at his fish.

"Hmmm," said Pap.

"I'd like to go see it," said Aaron.

"No," said Pap. This was an ongoing argument between them. Aaron wanted to see the end of the world for himself, but Pap knew in his heart that our farm was the only thing left seeing.

"He survived." Aaron gestured to Timor.

"Only because he knew enough to come here," said Pap.

"What do you think?" Aaron looked the stranger in the eye. "Could I survive out there?"

"I'd stay here if I were you." Timor's voice was a low purr. Jessup blushed at the sound of it.

"But what's out there?" Aaron pushed.

"Nothing that's not here, but better," he said. Even Pap blushed at that.

Timor stayed for a month. Then he stayed for two. The couch became his permanent home, and we tiptoed around him in the early morning. He ate everything we didn't want and helped with some of the hardest chores. He and Pap built a new goat pen. He helped Aaron fish, learned Mam's soda bread recipe, and showed me and Jessup how to make cheese from the goat's milk. He played with Pippa and tickled her until

12

she squealed. His face filled out and he looked less tired. We didn't know what the rest of the world was like, but here on the land that Timor was calling Spit's End, we had made a new family. We were the whole world.

Summer was creeping on, and I took to getting up earlier and earlier to milk the goats before they got to ornery from the heat. I got up at dawn, then just before, and finally when there were still stars. I would creep through the kitchen, past Timor's snoring form, and out to the pen, where I'd tell the goats about the dreams I'd had the night before.

One early morning when the moon was sinking I crept into the kitchen and heard voices. I stopped and listened, but couldn't make out any words, just soft goat-like noises. I thought maybe it was Aaron, preparing to finally leave; gathering some food to sneak away with. I peeked my head around the corner to stop him, but it wasn't Aaron.

I saw my sister's brown back, shiny in the soft light, perched atop the stranger's bulky lap. She rode him like a horse, like a wave, arching her back and hanging on as he moaned and groaned. She giggled silently, blushing pink in the semi darkness, her naked skin paling against Timor's dark hips and belly. He gave a last great lunge and lay still. Jessup climbed demurely off him, kissed him daintily on the cheek. She picked a bundle of clothing off the floor and scooted back to her room. Timor sighed once, loudly, and pulled our extra quilt back over his bottom half. He was wearing one of Pap's old button-down shirts.

I went back to my room. I was shaking. The goats would have to wait. I felt betrayed and lost and a little dirty. Breeding age—that was supposed to be a *joke*. Was Jessup too little to get that? Pap's snide remarks were not an invitation to climb aboard.

13

And then it occurred to me that maybe it had only been a joke when I said it, but not when Pap did. Maybe it had been a warning—correctly issued—and we should have locked Jessup in with the goats. But either way, what was I supposed to do about it? Timor was family now, but it wasn't like he was blood. And he clearly hadn't forced himself on Jessie in any way. She had been gushing about him non-stop since he first came to Spit Peninsula, and now it seemed he liked her too.

And then I wondered—what if I was next? Would he want to put his seed inside me too? Repopulate the world with tiny babies that were half him and half our women? What about Mam? And Pippa, when she was older? Would we be a baby farm along with goats and vegetables? It made me feel weird inside, half excited and half terrified. It was a big responsibility, being one of the mothers of the New World, but if that is what was expected of me, I would do it. My hands stopped shivering, so I went out to feed the goats.

I began to notice their absences. If I hadn't been looking for them, searching for a hint as to my future, I don't think I would have seen. But sometimes Mam would ask me to find Jessup, and it was like she had simply disappeared. Or Aaron would complain how Timor was supposed to help him with the fishing but he couldn't find him. Once I walked into the shed for some twine and there they were; both bottomless and sweaty. He had my sister's tiny body pinned up against the wall; her legs splitting in either direction around him as he grabbed onto her buttocks and pushed himself inside her. He was making that moan again, and she seemed to be getting at least some pleasure out of it; more than the female goats did when the males mounted them every year. I watched as Timor's round brown buttocks began to shake and pound more forcefully, and wondered how my sister didn't split in two.

14

I decided to come back for twine later.

After that, they were everywhere, like animals. In the grass, on the couch in the wee morning hours, down by the shore and doubtlessly in a hundred other places. It was worse to watch them than the goats. The goats didn't sweat and ignore me with self-absorbed smiles.

By October her belly had started to swell. She asked to borrow one of my loose dresses, and as she changed I saw it, and my breath caught.

"What?" she said crossly, but she was smiling.

"Can I tell you a secret?" She asked.

"No," I told her. "I'm busy."

"I've been busy too," she was sly, her eyes were sparkling. "I've been saving the world," she whispered, "Not just living in it."

"I know." I said. I threw another dress at her. "I saw you. I think it's disgusting. Pap's going to kill you."

Her smile fell, but only a little.

"He won't be mad. Once I have this little baby we won't be all alone anymore. The world will get so much bigger!" She held out her arms and fell backwards onto my bed; the dress gaping open where she hadn't yet buttoned it. The lump was smooth and shiny.

I knelt down next to her.

"Do you feel any different?"

"Oh, Cantor," her breath smelled like hayseed. "It's like I have the whole world inside me. The only one that matters. The new one."

I put my hand on the skin of her belly. It was warm.

"Did it hurt?" I asked.

"Not as much as the end of the world," she told me.

It took Pap a long time to notice, much longer than he would have had the goats been foaling. When he finally saw, it was late December and it was starting to snow. Jessup had just come inside, and was hanging up her coat on the hook by the door. When she leaned up, her shirt caught on something and pressed tight against her. Pap was standing at the sink.

"Jessup." He said, and the air stood still.

"Yes Pap?" She pulled her shirt down.

"Do that again." He said, and his voice was low and soft.

"Do what Pap?" Her eyes looked back and forth, all over the room, looking for Timor, or maybe me, or maybe just a way out.

He was over to her in three giant steps, grabbing her shirt roughly and pushing it up. She watched him, level, but her legs were shaking. Without a word, without taking his coat, Pap walked out the door. Jessup looked like she would fall, so I sat her on the couch.

"He will love me," she said, dazed, and I didn't know if she meant Timor or Pap.

There was a crack in the yard, and we ran to the window. Pap was standing in the snow with his shotgun, pointing directly at Timor, who had just come back from ice fishing with Aaron. My brother stood tall, confused. He looked old. Jessup screamed and tried to run to them, but I pulled her back inside and shut the door. We opened the window and knelt down beside it. She started weeping pitifully, leaking mucus down her pregnancy-swollen face.

Pap was shouting at Timor, but it wasn't words, it was a roar like the river in spring, when the ice began to break. Timor put his hands up just like in the movies we had watched before the electricity died. He dropped a line of fish into the snow, and Aaron crept behind him and picked them up, then ducked out of the way of Pap's waving gun.

16

"My daughter!" shouted Pap. "My daughter—" And he leveled the gun at Timor, who did nothing but watch. Apparently the first crack we'd heard had been no more than a warning.

Pap dropped to his knees. Snow puffed around him and his shoulders shook with sobs.

"I should cut off your balls." His voice was hoarse, it barked fiercer than Rosie. "You arrogant, selfish bastard. You take advantage of my hospitality, you take advantage of my daughter! I should kill you!" His sobs dried up, he was roaring again. The icicles on the roof above our window shuddered. He pointed the barrel of the gun into the ground and used it as a stick to pull himself back to standing.

"But we are the world. Killing you—killing you might be the greatest sin of all. You are an eighth of what's left." He paused for a moment and took a few breaths deep into his belly.

"Besides," he wiped snow and tears from his face with one woolly glove, "Besides, you and my daughter—what you made is my family. And maybe you done a good thing after all. Maybe a little baby is just what we need here at the end of the world." Pap loved to talk, but he wasn't usually much for serious speeches.

"It's not the end of the world." Timor's voice was low; we could barely hear it from inside the kitchen. He stuck his hand out to shake Pap's. "It's the beginning."

With another sob, Pap bypassed the hand and pulled Timor in for a great bear hug. Beside me, Jessup aged ten years and put a comforting hand on her belly, smiling through her tears. Aaron stood apart, his fish dangling from his hand. He saw us at the window. We locked eyes and I shook my head.

Pap and Timor came back inside, arms around each other like boys. They called for my mother and she came in from the bedroom, her face

17

wet too. She got out the oldest, most fermented cider and poured them each a glass. No one paid any attention to Jessup.

Later, Pap and Timor taught each other old drinking songs, and Pippa kept time by banging some spoons on the table. Mam couldn't stop smiling, and badly plucked some tunes on her old guitar. Jessup sat huddled on the couch, alternately beaming and scowling. Aaron swiped a bottle of cider and I followed him outside.

We went to the goat shed where it was warm with caprine breath. Aaron took a good long pull from the bottle and then handed it to me. It warmed me from the inside and made the edges of everything a little softer, easier to bear.

"It's not right," said Aaron quietly. I sipped fermented apples and waited for him to continue.

"You knew, didn't you?" It wasn't a question, but I nodded anyway.

"She loves him, I think," I said.

"What does it matter? He's the only one left. You'll probably be next." I shivered, thinking of Timor's bare buttocks drumming away in this very shed.

"I hope not." I said.

"Me too." Aaron gave me just a little smile.

"I know there's nobody else," I said, "But he's kind of... old, don't you think? Like, he's as old as Mam and Pap."

Aaron frowned again.

"But at least you have someone. Some option."

"What do you mean?" I asked.

"It's just—there's no one for me. And there's no one else coming."

"There's no one for me either." I said, and as soon as I did, the

18

weight of potential pregnancy was lifted off my shoulders. I didn't realize how worried I'd been; how much the thought of something growing inside me, especially something Timor had put there, scared me.

"Jessie can have him. I don't want him." I giggled, but Aaron was already talking.

"But what if there is, Cantor? What if there's someone else out there? What if there's someone for both of us?"

"No way," I told him, "You heard what Timor said. There's nothing left."

"Did he say it though?" Aaron took the cider from me. "Did you actually ever hear him say that?"

I thought back, and decided that I actually hadn't. Timor was quiet about the world outside Spit Peninsula. He never answered our questions with anything more than a tight lipped head shake. What had he seen out there? It must have been something terrible.

"I guess not." I said.

"Right," said Aaron, "And even if he had, he can't have been everywhere. Maybe there's another family, just like us, wishing there was someone else to meet."

"Do you want babies Aaron?" I took a large drink and swallowed a lot of air, started hiccupping.

"Well," he said, "I'd like to at least have the option." And I thought that was the funniest thing I'd ever heard, and I couldn't stop giggling. Soon we were lying on the floor amongst the goats, laughing big belly laughs. When we'd quieted, we lay in silence, listening to the goats chewing and mumbling in their sleep.

"I feel better," said Aaron.

"Me too." I said. I didn't even realize how bad I'd felt until that

19

moment.

We lay there in the hay, the world growing slow and dizzy and eventually lulled away into a pleasant melody of goats and snowfall.

That night I dreamed that a black and green snake crawled up between my legs and through all my insides to get to my belly, where it lay there, growing fat, waiting to be reborn. In the morning the world had turned to ice, and my head was pounding and my stomach ached.

Aaron made me coffee. Even though I never liked it before, that morning it dulled my head and warmed my feet and burned away any remaining snakes inside me.

Aaron had gathered up all his ice fishing gear and was cleaning it by the fire. Mam and Pap hadn't come out of their room yet, and Timor and Jessup were nowhere to be found. Pippa sat sleepily on my lap after a failed attempt at drinking my coffee, and I unraveled an old sweater so it could be re-knit into something new. Outside the snow whirled and whirled; not falling like the night before, but dry and screaming all around us.

"I think I want to leave." Aaron spoke softly, but his voice was loud in the quiet.

"Leave?" The idea was so utterly foreign to me that it punched a hole in my heart. "Where would you go?"

"Away. I don't know. It doesn't matter. Anywhere. Just to see."

"You can't leave now," I told him.

"Why not?" He wrapped fishing line around and around.

"Jessup's going to have a baby. It's snowing. Who would fish for us?" I gave him a babble of reason and Pippa shifted grumpily against me.

"When the snow stops," he said, "I'm going."

I felt chilled inside. I couldn't move, except to squeeze Pippa tighter to me.

"I only said this, because, do you want to come?" He polished his knife, not looking at me.

"Come?"

"With me. To see what's out there."

I thought about it. I thought honestly and hard. If Aaron left, there would be a bright spot of pain inside me. But if I left, I would be hollowed out, empty of all the things I knew. Either way was terrifying. Neither way felt right.

"I don't know," I said. There was a huge lump in my throat. I couldn't swallow, could barely speak around it.

"Think about it," he whispered, his voice like the blade he was sheathing. "When the snow melts, and Jessup's had her baby."

The winter was harsh, and squeezed us. Timor was an extra mouth to feed, unaccounted for until recently. Jessup had to eat more, even though she didn't want to, and Timor ate as though he were pregnant too. We often saw Mam slip part of her plate to Pippa's, and as a result Mam grew thinner and sharper; her face like brittle icicles pushed together. Pap was leaner too, not in his body but in his words. Timor ballooned around us all, sucking up our food and our spirits. Jessup's belly grew and grew, but she seemed to shrink behind it, until she was no longer a person but a vessel to hold this supposed new world. She crept into my bed at night and we traced her veins like continents. Timor ignored her. He was not harsh or rough; only distant and impartial now that that brush of fevered lust was gone.

His new target was Pap. He made our father teach him everything he knew, praising his every move and practically dog-licking him with subservience. It was worse to watch than his dalliances with Jessup. Pap would blush and stammer with the unusual attention and awkwardly praise Jessup for her choice in a man. He seemed to think Timor would be his charming son-in-law once the baby was born and time started again. He didn't notice that Timor had taken up Jessup's room and she had taken up mine, her belly all but shoving me out of the bed we now shared. Pap, when he spoke to us at all, spoke of a spring wedding, with lilacs and marigolds and the rush of the ice melt as background music. He gushed about refitting Mam's old wedding dress to fit Jessup. He was giddy as a school girl, giddier than the bride, who was not really a bride at all.

After a while I stopped listening to Pap, stopped believing everything would be okay again in the spring. This baby was not going to solve all of our problems. This wedding, if it even happened, wouldn't change a thing. Timor was slowly intruding on all of our lives, eating more of our food, and learning our ways only so he could change and control them.

I longed for spring, but only so I could escape the house and take the goats into the fields. Winter was a time for indoor work; mending and cleaning and preparing. We sat by the stove, immersed in our projects, listening to Timor tell us his grand plans for the future. He liked it warm too; warmer than we were used to, and warmer than was appropriate for our store of wood. He had no sweaters that fit him, he would explain, no coat and no warm clothes. I wanted to tell him if he ate less he would get smaller and fit it the clothes Pap gave him, but the silences from all around warned me not too.

I was stifled. I wanted to scream. I had never understood what cabin fever was before this winter. I couldn't speak, I couldn't breathe. Aaron was gone all the time; he had practically moved into the ice fishing hut.

He had promised me he would wait for spring, but I knew he walked farther and farther along the river every day. I was always afraid he wouldn't come back.

But it wasn't my greatest fear. My greatest fear was some unnamed beast of a thing, stronger than all the other fears jumbled up inside me. Whatever it was clawed to get to the top, and it paralyzed me. I jumped inside at every sound; I sweat through the night although Jessup stole the blankets. My hands shook and my lips were numb. I started sleeping in the hay in the goat shed. It was cold, but my bed was glacial with Jessup's moans and the feet that had begun to kick out from inside her.

And then Timor began to come to me in the night. He didn't do anything, just stood in the doorway, his enormous bulk shadowing the moon and blocking out the stars. He upset the goats, but I pretended to be asleep, though I wanted to shout and scream. Kale and Parsnip and the rest of them bleated blearily and formed a protective wall between us. Through my eyelid slit I saw him slowly shut the door and leave. In the morning I found the smallest, sharpest knife in the kitchen and took it to bed with me.

By March Timor and Jessup were hot air balloons of fat and child, and the rest of us were thin shadows in the night. Mam, especially skeletal, could see the bones in her wrists twist when she moved her hands. I never saw her eat anything anymore but the absolute last crusts and scrapings. Even when one of us tried to share with her she pushed it all away. The snow was beginning to melt, and when Timor came to watch me sleep he took up the whole doorframe.

And Jessup went into labor.

23

My former bed was soaked with blood and sweat. No one, of course, had any idea how to birth anything other than a goat. Mam helped because it was assumed that she would know the most about it. Jessup hadn't spoken a word in weeks, and I was afraid that when the baby came out it would snap her in half, and break Mam's wrists on its descent to the floor. If the baby looked anything like Timor it would be a huge mass that slid out of her. Its weight might crush us all.

Jessup cried throughout the entire labor. Mam fed her drips of water and put cold cloths on her head, but I was intensely worried that she would dry out before the baby came. I was used to the way goats gave birth; standing, seemingly suddenly, with little or no drama. The kid would practically fall out of its mother, who would help it stand in a matter of minutes. Baby humans took much longer and were much harder on everyone.

At last the head was visible and we all shouted "Push! Push!" because that's what we had read in books and seen on TV before the power died. The baby came out and it did not break Mam's hands or Jessup's hips or cause a huge crater in the floor with its weight. It didn't look like Timor; it didn't really look like anyone, just a wet squishy beast with a large voice that screamed and screamed.

"Shit," said Mam, "We need to cut the cord." Her eyes were wide and shiny. "How could I forget! Canter, run and get me a knife—" But I was already sliding my kitchen blade out of my long sock where I had hidden it. It wasn't sterile—but what was anymore? I sliced through Jessup's slippery flesh and shuddered at the thought that I was touching something that had been inside her moments before. She only blinked at me through her tears, and the baby only screamed, but Mam watched my face like she knew exactly why I had a knife in my sock. I shrugged my shoulders and wiped the blade off on the sheet; slipping the it back against my leg.

Mam wrapped the baby up in a towel and handed the bundle to Jess, who couldn't stop crying long enough to look at the thing that had come out of her.

"It's new world, Jessie," said Mam, turning Jessup's face to look at it, "And you made it." She didn't say anything about Timor.

That night we had a celebration, of sorts. The cider was so far fermented that it was hardly drinkable, but Pap and Timor had many toasts to each other and the world they were going to raise. We all crowded into my old room and Jessup smiled weakly up at us, but when she tried to kiss Timor he shied away with a look of revulsion. If anyone had had doubts of his lost interest in her, they were wiped clean away. Even Pap's jovial grin wavered for a moment, and you could almost see his spring wedding plans dripping off. But then he let out a roar of laughter and slapped Timor on the back, sloshing his cider onto the quilt.

"Boys will be boys!" He shouted nonsensically to the ceiling, almost loud enough to drown out his doubts.

If Timor had seen the knife in my sock, he hadn't said anything. In fact, he hadn't said anything to me since the first weeks he had come to us. He spoke to Pap, and Aaron, and presumably he had at least spoken to Jessup in the early days of their tryst. Pippa and I were invisible, and he spoke to Mam only when he wanted her to do something. He hadn't even asked anyone about the sex of his baby.

Jessup begged me to stay with her that first night, but I couldn't. She lay deep in exhaustion and the baby whuffled next to her, but I felt trapped and closeted inside that house. I missed the goat noises and the airy straw. I snuck back to the shed, and that's where Timor found me.

I was arranging my blanket on the ground when he opened the door. I froze, but I couldn't pretend to be asleep. Timor saw me and ducked his huge head under the doorframe. One of the goats scuttled out of his way and I tripped over it, falling back so I sat in the straw. Timor loomed over me like a childhood boogeyman.

"What do you want?" I asked, and I hoped my voice was loud and steady. He didn't answer me, but he came closer and closer; the moon blotting out the sun.

"Go away," I said, "Nobody wants you here." I sounded like Pippa when she whined.

"You want me." His voice was low and gravely, almost warm. "You all want me!" He grabbed my shoulders and wrenched me upward, and pain crinkled along my arms all the way down to my wrists. He shook me a little and my head rattled against the wall. I did not know if he meant to kiss me or kill me. He dropped me, and my vision wobbled. Big sausage fingers scrabbled at the waistband of my pants.

"Did the world even end?" I asked him. I could smell the cider on his breath. "Did anything happen out there?"

He tried to take down my jeans, but they caught up on the hilt of the knife. He shoved down harder and the tip of the blade went into my ankle and I screamed as loud as I could, fought as hard as I could, but I was so tiny and he was so huge and my shoulders and my ankle were against me, fighting me too, and it was no use, he would crush me and I would suffocate underneath him.

And then there was a sound like the river ice cracking in the spring; loud and sharp, and Timor gave a little grunt and fell to one side, toppling me and pinning my legs under him. There was another silhouette in the doorway behind him, small and frail and strong; my mother, with my father's shotgun.

She stepped over Timor and helped me stand. He blinked up at her with dazed eyes, darkness pooling wetly beneath him.

"You will not." She told him, the gun barely shaking in her hand as she pointed it at his throat. "And we will not. We will not be fooled by you, and kept by you. We took you in, and we fed you, and we clothed you, and you took advantage of everything we had." She pushed the muzzle into his throat. He tried to say something, but it was breathy and quiet and we couldn't make it out. She took my hand and pulled me roughly through the door.

Inside the house, everyone was awake.

"Timor's in the goat shed," she told Pap as we passed, then pulled me into the bathroom and locked the door.

My clothes, I noticed fuzzily, were covered in blood. Mam knelt down and began to undress me. I felt like a child again, like I was as little as Pippa, but I couldn't move or protest.

"Did he hurt you, Cantor?" I didn't answer, and she shook me. "Did he? It's important that you tell me—did he do anything to you?"

"No," I said, I whispered. Then "Thank you," came out clumsily, but I knew I had to say it.

Mam ignored me. She dipped a cloth in the bucket of water we kept for the sink and wiped off my legs. It was cold but felt good. I let her wash all of me, bandage my ankle, then I put on a sweater and some old pants and sat on the couch and drank a cup of putrid cider. Pap wasn't in the room. Pippa and Aaron came to sit on either side of me and held my hands.

"What do we tell Jess?" I asked, and my voice was a little hoarse.

"The truth." said Mam. She watched out the window, but no one

27

reappeared from the goat shed.

"Is Timor gonna be okay?" Pippa asked in her baby voice, the one she reverted to when she was scared or really wanted something.

Mam went over to her and stroked her fuzzy hair.

"Oh my love," she said, hugging Pippa to her stomach, "Everything is going to be okay. Everything is going to be so much better." Then she went to the kitchen and cut herself the biggest slice of soda bread we'd seen her eat in months.

Pap didn't come back until morning. Jessup napped with the baby, but the rest of us waited in our sentry positions around the stove. His face was dark and his eyes were tired. His footsteps dragged into the house. Aaron tensed beside me.

"It's done." Pap told us, but he only looked at Mam. "He's gone." He put his hat down on the table and went into his and Mam's bedroom, his boots leaving a slushy trail across the floor which Mam wiped up without a word of protest before she followed him.

Later, Aaron told me he'd seen something while he was fishing, way out in the middle of the river where the ice was too thin to set up camp. It looked like a body, swollen with death or stolen food. When he went back a few days later, the ice was melting and it was gone.

We all began to eat a little more, hoping the food would last until we could grow something again. We had to kill one of the goats for meat, and I tried not to show everyone that I was crying. The house was quieter. It was like we had forgotten the habit of speech.

The baby was loud, too loud, it cried and laughed and screamed and babbled in a roar as big as the ocean. Jessup watched it blankly, as if she didn't know what it was. Mam changed the baby and burped it, but

28

she couldn't feed it. She and Jessup would go into my room for long periods of time to try to nurse, and sometimes Jessup would cry along with her baby. Mam would come out exhausted, and Jessup expression wouldn't change. No one went into the room Timor had slept in.

And one day, just like I knew he would, Aaron disappeared. He took a soda bread Mam had baked the night before and some fishing gear, and left without a word. No one cried for him. Everyone knew what was coming. Pap began to curse at Aaron's selfishness and lack of foresight, but Mam said "I thought boys would be boys?" sharp as a slap, and Pap shut up after that. His grammar got better too.

Aaron's absence was hard on all of us. No one else had the patience for fishing like he did, and I started setting baited lines as traps without much hope. We planted seeds and weeded and lugged water from the river to sprinkle over the seedlings. Jessup sat inside at the window looking like an old woman. Sometimes Mam left the baby on a blanket in the sun while she worked.

Pippa had a growth spurt and she looked like a bird; her legs like a heron's and her arms like skinny wings. She still danced and chattered and whined like a child, as though she didn't remember Timor at all.

When summer came and the baby learned to smile, Mam decided he needed a name. We had all been tiptoeing around Jess, not asking her any questions, not pushing things on her. But enough was enough.

"Ben," said Jessup, and began to cry again, but this time I cried too, because I remembered the original Ben, our neighbor to the west who we had not heard from since well before the world ended. He was a kind, quiet man a little older than our parents, who had a shiny black sheepdog that trailed him everywhere. We used to pick berries on his property.

"Baby Ben," Mam said, and picked him up so his legs were

29

dangling. Pippa poked him in the stomach and he kicked and laughed. We didn't laugh with him, because we were broken.

When Baby Ben began to walk, Jessup did too. She followed him around the house with just the tiniest glimmer of an expression on her face. Eventually she took his hands and walked with him outside, past Pap in the garden, past my goat shed, down to the river. I had a sudden, insane fear that she was going to throw him in and let him wash away, and I followed her.

They moved slowly. Ben's legs were tiny, and Jessup hadn't walked further than the length of the house for over a year. She was talking to him, actually talking, in voice so low that I couldn't understand the words. At the river, she knelt in front of him, like Mam had done for me the night Timor died, and took off his tiny shoes and his tiny pants. Then they walked to the edge of the water and she swung him with both of her hands in a wide, sunny arc. Just as I was preparing to run my hardest and dive in to save that baby, she brought him down so just his toes were skimming the water, then his feet, then his ankles, then he was standing in the river with his hands in hers, high over his head. He squealed and squeaked and giggled, and suddenly Jessup laughed too, surprised at herself. Baby Ben looked alarmed for a second, and she pulled him up above her head, and he kicked water droplets down on her like rain. Maybe he was the new world, after all.

When Aaron came home, we were laughing in the kitchen, all of us. How strange our voices must have sounded to him from outside the door. We were different from the family we'd left, but maybe more like the family we'd remembered. He walked in without a word or a knock, set his backpack down with a loud thump, and everything stopped, except Pippa, who was singing a song to Ben to make him eat his oatmeal and whose back was to the door. Her voice wavered on in the silence for a moment, and then she said "What?" and turned around.

He looked a little taller, and he had a short, bristly beard. He was wearing a brown coat I didn't recognize, and he was very dirty. No one spoke. What could we say?

Ben, finally deciding he wanted to eat, banged his spoon on the table and said "More" in a very clear voice. Aaron's eyes widened a little. The silence ticked on.

It was Pap who broke it. He shouted "My boy!" and grabbed Aaron in a bear hug and started to sob. Ever since Jessup and Ben had discovered it was okay to laugh again, Pap had found it was okay to cry too, and he used it at every opportunity. Aaron hugged him back and Ben cried in solidarity with Pap.

The cider had just been bottled the week before, so nothing was fermented yet, but we took it out for a traditional family celebration. Mam and Pap wanted to cook a welcome-back feast, but Aaron had something else in mind. His backpack, which had made such an unnaturally loud noise when he had dropped it on our floor, was full of canned food. Carrots, peas, lentil soup. There was curry and tomato paste, tuna and lamb. Aaron had packed years of preserves into one small backpack.

They spilled out onto the table. Jessup lunged for the tuna, but no one else moved. I saw Mam and Pap exchange a look that said more than any words, more than almost five years of isolation, of farming and fishing and togetherness.

"The world hasn't ended, has it?" I said, because no one else would. Aaron shook his head.

"It's still there," he said, and his voice was still my brother's.

No one laughed, and no one sobbed.

"But what about—" Pap's voice trailed off.

"What does it even matter?" said Aaron. He sounded tired. "It's all there, more or less. It's not pretty, but there's other people, and food, and some other stuff. There's other people, Cantor." He looked at me, but I turned away. I couldn't tell if I was angry at him for leaving me here, or for bringing the rest of the world back. I went and found the forgotten can opener so I wouldn't have to see him.

Mam and Pap wanted to ration the cans out, make them last as long as possible, but Aaron said "What's the point? We can always get more." and so we had a feast.

Afterwards, my stomach heavy from the unaccustomed richness of the meat and sauces, I went to sit outside. I had moved into Aaron's room after he left, but thought I might sleep in the goat shed again now that he was back. The stars were bright and it was cold, the clear cold of early fall. I could feel winter creeping closer. The goats could feel it too; they rustled and bleated louder to keep it away.

The shed felt small and too full. There had been a few more babies since I'd last slept out here, and I was bigger too. If I tried really hard, I could see the stain on the floor where Timor had rested. I ran my hands over the walls to see if my head had made any indentation, but I couldn't find one. I shuffled the straw around, but couldn't get comfortable. The goats grumbled louder and shot me angry glances through their creepy alien eyes.

When the knock came at the door it was a relief. I knew he would come to me, was that why I had moved out here? I didn't know if I wanted to hug him or hit him, or if the truth was somewhere in between.

"What?" I said to the closed door that now could lock from the inside as well as out.

I thought of his bearded face and the strange familiarity of him. He looked like me, but he walked a little different and he talked a little different. He was full of newness and outside-ness, but at the core we were the same. We had shared the same womb, the same house, the same voice. He was coming to ask me to leave with him.

But when he didn't answer or knock again, I got worried. What if my long lost brother was gone again? What if he had left without me?

I threw open the door, and there was a can of coconut milk at my feet. Before, I had loved coconut milk, had loved anything sweet. Aaron, my only brother, had remembered that. He had remembered me from out there in the world.

I took the can back in and locked the door, then found a screwdriver and banged a hole in the lid.

The milk was sweet and did not sit well in my stomach, but I kept drinking it, hoping that if I had enough I would like it again. I thought of the night Aaron and I had gotten drunk in the shed and the world spun around us; when we were the axis. I felt dizzy just thinking about it.

When the second knock came, I was ready. I didn't wait; I might not have another chance. I almost knocked over the can in my hurry to slide the lock, down and to the right.

But it wasn't Aaron. It was my mother.

Her nightgown glowed in the moonlight, and her boots stuck out from underneath.

"Oh," I said, "Hi." As far as I knew, she hadn't been out here since that night with Timor.

I could see her trying not to look at the straw I had brushed over the floor stain.

"Come on," I said, and she did. I locked the door behind her, just in case.

"I saw Aaron come out here," she said.

"He brought me coconut milk." I picked up the can, and the watery liquid sloshed inside. "Want some?"

She shook her head. "Never liked the stuff."

I could remember her drinking it, and giving it to me to drink.

I sat down in the straw, and she awkwardly sat down across from me. She moved like an old woman, like her bones were brittle and hurt. She had put her weight back on once Timor was no longer eating her share, but the careful effort had made her body tired and face lined.

"You should go."

"But I like it out here." I didn't really. I was just defiant, angry at her and Pap, angry at Aaron, angry at the outside world which had the nerve to continue on without us.

"No," she said, and for a moment I thought she could see right through me and read my mind. "You should go," she said again, took a deep breath, "With him. With Aaron."

A flashy spark of panic went off deep within my belly.

"He's leaving? Already? He just got here!" Suddenly all was forgiven, I wanted nothing more than to talk to him, catch him before he was gone again.

"Not yet." She looked down, shuffled the hay with her feet. "But he will. Before the weather turns."

"I can't," I said, and my voice sounded so small and young, younger even than Pippa's. "This is my home."

Mam looked at me, locked her eyes with mine with a steel force. I wanted to move, but I couldn't break her gaze.

"Is it?" she asked, and I couldn't move. She snaked forward and grabbed the can from my stone fingers, tossed the rest of the milk back

34

in a single gulp. And she was gone, unlocking the bolt so fast I barely saw it.

In the morning, I milked the goats and left the shed early. The sun was bright and cold and I could feel the frost wanting to set on the ground. Only a few more weeks and it would.

I opened the door quietly and snuck in with my pail of milk, but Aaron was already awake.

"I made you coffee," he said, which for some reason made me angry.

"How come," I slammed the pail on the counter, sloshing a little over the sides, "everybody in this house knows me so much better than I do?"

Aaron shrugged, sheepishly, quietly, and I wanted to hug him and shake him all at once, even more than I ever did to my other siblings. I poured some coffee and sat down across from him.

"No milk?" he asked.

"No." I was thrilled—here was something he didn't know about me! Something that had changed without warning while he was away!

"I drink it black now," I said.

He laughed, and I flicked a crumb across the table at him.

"Shut up."

"You shut up."

I flicked another, and it landed in his beard. He brushed it away, and I saw he'd cleaned his nails sometime in the night.

"It's new." He gestured to a dented looking can on the counter. "I thought you might enjoy something fresh after all this time reusing grounds.

It was almost too fresh and I gagged on the taste for a moment, torn

35

between drinking it black and adding goat's milk and proving him right.

"Who's out there?" I asked. I wouldn't know any of them, but that wasn't the point. "Tell me their names."

"There's Marin," he started, and wondered if she was special. I felt a little jealousy creeping in. "Tom," he continued, "Andew J., Peter, May, Amelia." He said their names like he was reading a bible, and I listened to his sermon, reverent in the quiet kitchen of our childhood home.

When he was finished I had drunk my coffee without noticing. All I could see was their faces, imagined and real at the same time.

"Is it bad out there?" I asked.

"Is it better here?"

I didn't know the answer. He opened a can of smoked fish, and I couldn't tell if it tasted fresher or flatter than the fish we smoked ourselves, but I still ate the whole thing, because it was different.

Aaron stood up. He was already wearing his boots, boots that I had never seen on him before. He picked up his rucksack and added cider, soda bread, goat cheese, and left all the remaining cans in a neat stack next to the sink.

"Aren't you going to say goodbye?" A lump was forming in my throat, and it was hard to talk.

"Already did. Years ago." He went to the door, lifted the latch.

"Are you coming?"

My breath caught, and I thought of my sleeping family, dreaming all around me, breathing the same air we had breathed for the last five years. Like the fish, I couldn't tell the difference between stale and fresh. Was anything better, new or old? Safe at home or in the unknown? There might be more Timor's there, but there were also

Toms, Amelias, Andrew J.s. And Marins. And Aarons.

I shrugged my shoulders, tossed back the fresh coffee grounds at the bottom of my cup like they were nothing.

"Okay."

Sturgeon and Petrel

We were born at home. According to my mother, it was because the sea that day raged fiercely in anticipation of our coming. There was no less than a hurricane, a whirlpool, and waves the size of a school bus. The roads were flooded, apparently symbolically, as was the truck's transmission. My mother gritted her teeth like her Viking ancestors and lay down in the bathtub to have us out.

According to my father, my mother is overdramatic. The truck was broken, as was often the case, and it was raining. He offered to call an ambulance or even take her around to the neighbor's by boat, but she locked herself in the bathroom, not to emerge until we were born. Or until my father, tired of hearing screams and realizing the pot of water he had been instructed to boil was nothing more than a distraction, broke down the door. To this day, none of the rooms in the house have locks.

My father was too late in his heroics to witness our birth, and as a result of these strange circumstances my mother is the only one who knows which of us came out first, a fact which she has never revealed.

My mother also likes to tell us that we were named after the two animals that washed ashore during our birthing. The story goes that Mother, never one to let something as insignificant as two large babies being ripped from her body slow her down, took a nap until the storm passed and then went out to weed the garden. Once there, she found a dead petrel and a dead sturgeon, clinging together among the wreckage of the tomato vines.

"Harry," she called to my father, "start up a soup." Then she plucked the bird and deboned the fish and she and my father ate root-vegetable-and-twin-daughter soup and named their offspring after,

38

basically, road kill.

I tend to doubt this story because Sturgeons are mainly freshwater fish, and that would have had to have been some storm to wash them all the way up here. My father denies it fervently and turns a little green when my mother talks about the soup, but he only mumbles incoherently and changes the subject whenever we asked about our strange names.

We must have been terrible babies. We were terrible children and terrible teenagers, so one can only imagine what we were like before we were able to talk and pout and sulk under our own power. We probably screamed like seagulls and cried like a summer storm. Mother claims that when our hair came in in it grew straight up like dune grass, waiting until we were almost two to finally flop over and follow the path gravity had already set. Father says that when we teethed he gave us frozen seaweed and our baby lips stained blue as the water, our breath smelling of salt and sand and musk. The only photographic proof of our babyhood shows us small and blurry, crawling out of an obviously posed picture by the tree outside the front door. In it, Mother smiles with her lips pressed tight together, staring straight at the camera as if daring it to question her parenting skills. Father, standing stiffly in his rarely used dress shirt, has spotted our mischief out of the corner of his eye just as the shutter clicked.

As children we were no less dramatic. Petrel was moody and I would whine. We would take turns following our mother around the house and throwing ourselves down dramatically on various pieces of furniture, sighing loud enough to compete with the surf.

"Why can't we go into town today?" one of us would ask, either morose or dripping with petulance.

"Because," my mother would explain, "the truck needs new tires (or

39

new transmission, or brakes—the list was endless) and your father is out on the boat. Why don't you go outside and play with your friends?"

"But we don't have any friends," we would yowl.

My mother would fix us with one of her Viking warrior glares. The glare meant the argument was over. We didn't have to agree with her, but she knew she was right and we knew we had to do whatever she said or be met with a fate worse than a simple stare.

"You have each other," she would say, the cold firmness of each word slicing through our protests.

Mother didn't understand. We may have had each other, but that didn't mean we liked each other. We only tolerated each other *because* we had no one else. We would quarrel, always. We would fight over small things and large things and nothings. A fight usually started with yelling and escalated to sand throwing, hair pulling, and once, dramatically, when Petrel pushed me too hard and I tripped over a driftwood log, a black eye.

The black eye fascinated us. For once, people could tell us apart. Mother and Father feigned anger at first, and Petrel was punished of course, but I think secretly they were relieved. For two solid weeks, we weren't identical. We would stand at the mirror and watch ourselves, fascinated as the skin around my eye turned from red to purple to yellow. We would feel the swollen area, tracing the soft tender skin at the top of my cheekbone and comparing it to the tighter skin on Petrel's face.

Other than that temporary mark, we looked exactly alike. Every freckle and hair and fingernail was completely the same. We didn't dress alike, but since Mother only saw fit to provide us with a limited number of clothes, we swapped them back and forth so many times that we might as well have. Father would suggest periodically that one of us

40

cut our hair short, and we both argued that it should be the other sister who did it. Mother, normally the enforcer on matters such as these, was sentimental about our hair and didn't even like to trim it for us.

Once the black eye faded, things went back to normal and no one could tell who was who. Mother claimed she could, but we both knew she was lying. Even I couldn't tell us apart. We would still stand in the bathroom and look in the mirror but now we looked like an army of clones, a repeating pattern reflected back and forth forever. I would stare at the image on the right and know it was me, but it could have just as well have been her. If I moved my arm, the girl on the right moved her arm, but what if we had switched places and I just hadn't noticed? If Petrel did something bad and I was blamed, sometimes I would get confused. Had I done it? If another little girl who looked and talked and moved just the way I did knocked that pitcher of water off the table and didn't clean it up, who is to say it wasn't me? It might as well have been. I probably had this identity crisis for years, and maybe always would have, if Petrel hadn't almost drowned.

It was August, and it was hot. We were bickering more than usual; about who was hotter, who wanted to go swimming more, and who was more excited about entering a real school in the fall. My mother, at last unable to stand the sound of screechy child-voices, put on her Viking death stare and told us to "go get acquainted with our namesakes," which either meant "go play on the beach" or "go play dead." Either way, whenever she brought up the source for our unusual names in a non-romantic way, we knew it was time to leave and give Mother some alone time.

We went down to the beach, like we always did. It was either the beach or the scraggly crop of pine trees we called "the woods," but neither of us liked the woods. The underbrush was so heavy that, instead of cooling relief in the shade, the foliage knitted together a greenhouse of trapped air where every mosquito for miles around would come for an afternoon nap. Petrel and I both had masses of long dark hair, which not only trapped bugs and dirt and pine needles but added another layer to the greenhouse. The beach was hot, and the sand burned our feet, but at least there were no mosquitoes and we could stand in the water. We were both excellent swimmers but weren't allowed in further than our knees without direct adult supervision. My father liked to point out that it was possible to drown in an inch of water, to which my mother would always counter by telling him that we were children, not idiots, and did he want to supervise us in the bath as well? Every time we got a drink? Father won on this one though, and the knee rule always stayed.

The water was cold. It was always cold no matter how hot the weather was; it was shocking and bone biting, and after only a few minutes our feet went numb. Sometimes we stuck our hands in, and sometimes our hair, but we always obeyed the "not beyond the knees" rule. But that August was so hot that Petrel decided that just over the knees wasn't breaking any kind of rule. And I followed her, because the water was so cold and the air was so hot, and because if I didn't, she said she'd tell Mother I took off all my clothes and went swimming. But when she went in so deep that she had to hold her shorts up around her waist, I stopped even though she threatened me. I was more afraid of Mother than I was of Petrel, so I watched like a good little girl while she waded in deeper and deeper, finally letting go of her shorts and allowing the legs to billow up around her.

"Look at me!" she cried, waving her arms around her head, "Look at meeeee!" And all of a sudden she was gone.

"Very funny, Peter Petrel." I said, splashing waves in the direction

42

she had disappeared.

"Pee-Pee Petrel," I said, which is what I called her when only she could hear. It always made her mad and I was sure she'd burst up screaming right in front of me. I was kind of jealous she had gone swimming without me, even though I knew we weren't supposed to.

But when she didn't come up for air, even when I teased and splashed and called her names, I started to get worried. If she was gone, who was I? Which one of us would the mirror's reflection show? So I balanced Mother's rage at me coming home wet and me coming home without Petrel, and I dove in the water.

It was cold, and my brain sliced open for a second, but then my whole body was numb and I pushed forward, scooping the water with my cupped hands and pretending they were fins like Father had taught me. Petrel was right there on the bottom, floating a little but not moving or kicking. Not even when I slammed into her. I grabbed her arms and pulled her back to the surface. The water wasn't even deep; it came barely to the bottom of my rib cage.

"Petrel," I said, "Stop playing. It isn't funny anymore. Petrel! Peter Petrel, Pee-Pee Petrel!" I shook her and I dragged her back to the beach and when I dropped her in a heap on the sand, she started coughing, and then she threw up, something Petrel and I never did. We had strong Viking stomachs. She opened her eyes and looked right at me, and there was something different in those eyes. Something I had never seen in my own reflection. She hissed at me and screamed like a bird, and I slapped her right in the face and she stopped.

"Stee," she said. She always called me Stee, and I felt bad for a moment and resolved not to call her Pee-Pee any more. "I almost drowned."

"I know." I told her. "You were floating like a dead fish."

43

"Woah." she said. Her eyes were so wide.

"I saved you," I told her.

"You did?"

"You almost drowned," I said again, "But I saved you. I went in and got you out."

And then Petrel started laughing, and the water dripped out of her nose and her hair, and out of her new eyes. And I laughed with her, even though I wasn't really sure what was funny.

And that was the first time the sea tried to take Petrel.

We didn't tell Mother what had happened. We played on the beach, together for once, until our clothes dried enough to go home. Our hair was stiff and salty and we had to have a bath, but as we often stuck our hair in the sea to cool off no one thought anything of it.

Petrel was different after her near death experience. For the rest of the summer she was quieter and would often stand in the water and stare out to sea like she was thinking. I refused to go wading with her and actually became a little bit suspicious of the ocean; sometimes I would have nightmares where the waves tried to steal my feet, and it made me wary to go in even in the daytime. We got along better for the rest of August, mostly because Petrel refused to fight. Sometimes I would call her "Pee-Pee Petrel," my earlier resolve quickly forgotten, or throw sticks at her, just to get her attention, and we would fight halfheartedly before she would stop and go all thoughtful again.

On our first day of school, we stood side by side at the mirror while Mother brushed our hair. There was no doubt in my mind which girl was me and which was my sister.

We went to a tiny coastal school which held all children in the area up to fifteen years old. After that students travelled further inland for high school, unless they dropped out to work on the boats like my father did. We had to trek almost half a mile to the bus stop because the district refused to let the bus drive on our unpaved road. Mother marched us to the end and unceremoniously deposited us on the bright yellow bus, probably relieved that she could finally get some rest now that her twin terrors were out of range for seven or eight hours every day.

In school, no one could tell us apart. It was even worse than at home; at least Mother and Father tried. People at school couldn't even remember our names. We got called "the bird girl" and "the other one—the fish one." Our teacher sat everyone alphabetically by last name and refused to change the order so we could be apart. At recess we ate lunch together but alone under a big pine tree. We might as well have been at home.

On the bus ride back I cried and cried and Petrel refused to talk to me. She looked out the window and smiled that new serene smile and I decided that I hated her, and wished she had drowned. Mother picked us up at the bus stop, looking fresh and relaxed, and I howled into her arms that I wanted to stay home with and play on the beach and have things just like they used to be.

"Not on your life," said Mother, and marched us back home.

That night, I decided it was time for drastic measures. I got a lemon slice and Mother's kitchen scissors and waited until Petrel was asleep, biting down on the lemon whenever I felt tired and letting the squirt of sour juices jolt me back awake. By the time I was sure she was sleeping I was so anxious I had chewed my lemon to a pulp, and my stomach felt acidic and jittery. I picked up the scissors and cut off a good six inches of Petrel's hair.

When I went to throw them away, I was struck by that strange feeling again; like I was holding my own hair in my hands and had accidentally given myself the dreaded haircut. It felt so heavy and so exactly like my own that it almost seemed to be alive. Could we grow another sister out of it? Water it and plant it in the ground and have another twin? And what would her name be—Petunia or Raccoon or Great White Shark? I couldn't risk it. Everybody knows that trash sometimes turns to compost, and compost is the same thing as the dirt in the garden. I tied the hair in a big knot, slipped it inside a sock, and hid it under my bed.

In the morning, I woke to Petrel screaming. She was serene no longer. She didn't stare out windows or refuse fights or think about the sea. She jumped on top of me and hit me in the face and tried to strangle me before Mother came and pulled us apart. She was angry, Petrel was angry, but I was smiling. I had my sister back, but now we were different again. It was like the black eye but better—longer lasting, closer to permanent.

Petrel looked like a mangy dog and sulked until Mother evened out what was left of her hair. She didn't look that bad, but I looked better.

"Maybe I'll be a hairdresser," I said.

"Maybe you'll drop dead."

In school, I shined. People may not have remembered my name, but they knew I was the sister with the long hair. At recess Petrel and I sat under our tree again, but a few girls joined us. And at the end of the day, when I forgot my lunch bag and had to run back inside, my teacher said "Goodbye Sturgeon" as I was leaving.

She said my name! She knew which sister I was! For that moment, alone in the empty classroom, I glimpsed myself as an individual for the first time. Instead of Sturgeon-not-Petrel, I could just be Sturgeon. I

46

could be myself: a single sister, identical to no one. Who knew what I could accomplish as just myself?

And then in the morning, I woke up with a new haircut.

It was shorter than Petrel's. It was less even, and more chunks stuck up. I had a mohawk, a cowlick, a spitcurl, a pixie cut, all on the same head. I screamed at her. She screamed back that I had started it. We hit, we fought, we punched. Hair flew, scissors flew, Petrel's palm was sliced open just as Mother came in. She slapped us. Hard. Little girl fists were no match for a single, well-aimed blow from a fully grown woman with iron in her bones. We stopped crying. We stopped making any noise at all.

"This. Has. To. Stop." said Mother. We knew how to read, we could hear the capital letters in each word.

"There will be no more hair cutting. There will be no fighting. If you two cannot get along, there will be no school. I will teach you myself, and you will work on weekends with your father on the boat."

It was the ultimate threat. It accomplished more than countless Viking stares ever could. School, and other people that came with it, were the only thing we had ever wanted. No matter how much we said we hated it, for six hours a day we could be away from our little beach house, and theoretically away from each other. If Mother taught us, like she had for the past two years, we would never get out. We would spend the rest of our lives standing in water almost up to our knees and swatting bugs. We would help Father on his fishing boat and weed the garden, grow old and eventually die and be buried in the woods. We would never meet new people, and our haircuts would be in vain.

"We'll be good." We promised.

Of course, as much as we wanted to meet new people, we had no idea how to act around them. We tried different approaches: Petrel would be quiet and listen to the other children as much as she could; I would ask them never ending questions. She would chase after them at recess while I would sit under our tree and wait for someone to come and talk to me. It wasn't so much that the other children disliked us, they just didn't know what to do with us. We would arrive at school with our haircuts spiked up around our faces (me) or in a huge frizzy cloud (Petrel), and our clothes would switch seemingly indiscriminately between us. We would scream and fight, and then be silent. We knpw how to read and do simple arithmetic but had no knowledge of geography or history aside from the Viking war stories and Irish seafaring legends our mother and father told us. We were odd, and the other children knew it first. Our first year in school we learned there would only be the two of us, forever. We struck up a grim reluctant friendship based on the idea that no one else wanted us.

The second time the sea nearly took Petrel we were almost twelve. There was a hurling gale, just like there was every year near our birthday. Mother said it was because the sea remembered us and wanted us back; Father said it was because it was storm season. This time, at least, Mother turned out to be right.

The storm started around dinner time. We were eating fish, which was normal, and strawberry preserves on biscuits, which was normal, and chocolate flowers, which was definitely not normal. My father had bought them in town as a near-birthday treat for us—which made it doubly strange; my father had bought food, instead of catching or growing or trading for it, and he had gone into town to do so. My father rarely went into town, and when he did it was not to buy something frivolous like chocolate covered flowers.

They were delicious. The chocolate disintegrated almost

48

immediately, leaving a velvet petal with a summer taste. We ate them silently, savoring each strange bite.

There was one flower left in the middle of the table, and we were all wondering who was going to get it when the storm started. At first it was only little raindrops, *plinging* against the windows and sounding innocently like an unwinding music box. Father crossed his knife and fork over his empty plate and the rain began to fall in earnest. Mother jumped up from the table and went to get the rags she used to stuff up the gaps in the sills and we knew it was going to be bad. Mother could feel a storm from miles away; and if she ever asked Father not to go out on the boat on a particular day, he always listened.

Father ran out to bring the dinghy further up onto shore, and Petrel and I went with him. We'd made it halfway down the beach before I heard Mother calling after us for someone to help her with the garden, so I turned back. We pulled some old sheets taut between us and stretched them over the plants, pounding stakes into the corners in hopes that the wind would have pity on our food source and leave them where they were. Mother was rounding up stray trowels and pots when I felt a cold slice in my brain like on the day I had pulled Petrel out of the water. The cold moved all the way down into my chest, then my gut, and I threw up all over the sheet in front of me.

All the chocolate, I thought bleakly, and Mother took my arm and pulled me back inside. I was covered in mud, and she wrapped me in towels and got me a drink of juice.

"What's wrong?"

I couldn't even answer. I was freezing all over and couldn't seem to process her words. She sat me at the table and smoothed back my hair, now grown long again, and all my eyes could focus on was that last chocolate covered flower. And then, like something out of a novel, the door banged open and my father stood there, dark hair streaming wet and beard uncurling, holding my limp sister in his arms.

Nobody moved until my hand reached toward the chocolate covered flower on its own.

"Is she—" my mother asked.

Father dropped my sister on the couch, dropped her roughly, and I knew she wasn't dead. She sputtered weakly, and we were eight again, me dragging her to shore on that still August afternoon. Through the ice in my brain I forced my way to her and pulled her shoulders up so she was sitting and hit her as hard as I could across the back. Water frothed out of her nose and she slumped forward and said "Ow, Stee-vee," and all that ice melted and I started breathing normally again.

In all the drama of the storm and the ocean's second try on my sister's life, everyone forgot about the last piece of chocolate. When it was quiet again, I wrapped it in a napkin and put it under the bed with Petrel's hair.

This time, I didn't have any dreams, but Petrel did. She moaned and thrashed for three nights. She wet the bed. She cried for hours and shuddered when she tasted the salt of her tears. I tried to comfort her or fight her, but she didn't want me. Suddenly, my own sister was as mysterious as the minds of our schoolmates.

She and Father had been pulling the dinghy onto the beach when the sea began to get rough. The waves were suddenly huge, and the lightening was raging. Father was knee deep in the water and told Petrel to wait—they might hit a sink hole, but the thunder and the waves were too loud and she couldn't hear. She tried to keep going and Father tried to stop, and waves caught the little boat and it flew out of his hands and struck her in the shoulder. She went down, and the boat went over her, nearly taking Father with it. He wrestled with it like a

Viking and saw the bubbles where my sister struggled. He found her in water up to his shoulders, and she wasn't breathing. The boat floated away and he let it, dragging my almost dead sister toward the shore. He pushed the water from her lungs and saw the waves coming; huge waves which maybe had her name on them. That's when he picked her up and ran for home, and I fought the last bit of sea out of her.

It was like our squabbles had been working towards this moment. Every time I hit her, I made us stronger. When she fought me, she was the sea fighting me back. We were stronger than the ocean, if we fought together.

Petrel changed again after the storm. She didn't stare serenely out the bus window thinking about death and life and the ocean. She curled up in the corner of her bed farthest from the window and refused to come out. She called me names and screamed at Mother. The only one she would let near her was Father, and only to bring her food. She refused to eat anything that came from the sea, resembled the sea, or was salty. This meant no soup, no fish, no water. She ate what she deemed "earthy foods;" bread and vegetables and juice. She was most fond of turnips, carrots and other things that spent the majority of their lives underground. She talked about wanting to move inland, away from the sea. It seemed that, for the first time, my sister was afraid.

Being frightened was simply something that had never occurred to us before. We were safe in our little house with our parents who provided for us. We had our school, which was strange, and the other children, who had grown to tolerate us, if not actually like us. Our world was tiny and protected, we were bull-headed like Mother and resourceful like Father, and we had never thought about the fact that there was something out there that we would need protection from. The only thing that had ever been able to hurt us before was each other.

Petrel was afraid, so I felt that I should be afraid—but I wasn't sure how. My sister refused to leave our room, but I went to look for things to be frightened of. I snuck out of the house at night and went into the woods to see if I was afraid of the dark like some of my schoolmates. I wasn't. I was annoyed by the mosquitoes and then cold from the wind. I was scratched and bruised and overly tired the next day, but I wasn't afraid.

I tried walking into town by myself, but that wasn't frightening. It was boring and lonely. My feet hurt. There was nothing to do in town without Petrel there to keep me company, so I walked back. Again, I was tired but not afraid. I went to our room, sat on my bed, and thought about what it all meant. What were the other kids frightened of? Bugs, spiders, the dark; bears and monsters and being up high. But I could think of a logical defense for each one of them, except heights. I had never tested that fear before. Petrel and I had given up climbing trees when were grew tired of tangling our hair with sap and being bitten by the ever present bugs, and we had been too little to get very high. If I went up far enough, could I feel what Petrel felt? Maybe if I could combine all her fears, I would finally understand. I curled up into the corner of my bed like she did, watched her breathing under her blanket, timing the rise and fall of my chest to hers.

"Peter," I said, "Peter Petrel." She didn't move. "Is it the ocean that you're afraid of? Or water in general?"

She was quiet for a long moment, but her breathing had changed and it was listening breathing.

"The ocean," she finally said. "But not the ocean itself. It's what the ocean's made of. You know?"

"Okay," I said, though I didn't really get it. I got off of my bed and started changing into my swimsuit. "I'm going to go find it."

She came out of her blanket. She looked greasy, not having been able to bathe since the incident.

"What are you doing to do?"

"I'm going to find the scary part of the ocean. I'm going to find out what you're so afraid of." I slipped the cool fabric over my legs. It gave me goosebumps.

"Don't." She said. She wasn't whining, or whimpering, or nagging like the before-Petrel. She just said "Don't" very flatly. And I felt something—not scared, exactly, but a little unsure. This was unfamiliar territory. I was going off to do something, not only without my sister, but something that she had told me not to do. Not that she was going to tell on me, or hate me, or hit me. Just:

"Don't." She said it again and there was a little edge of panic to her voice, and it made a little thrill run up my body. I put on some shorts and my sneakers and backed out of the room so I could watch her the whole way, just in case she tried to stop me. She didn't. She just sat on the bed, skin shiny in the pale light, whispering "Don't" in capital letters like our mother.

Outside, I went to the woods, but I didn't go into them. I walked the outer perimeter along the cliff face looking for the perfect tree, and when I found it I climbed it. Halfway up, my hands began to sting, and the wind whipped at my hair and eyes, making tears run down my face. I tasted them and thought of the ocean and Petrel back indoors saying "Don't" and all the children at school, afraid of snakes and bats and having no one to talk to. And I pushed myself up to the very top, and I jumped.

Falling was like breathing out, very suddenly. There was no air inside me, only around me, whooshing by and catching my skin and hair with pine needles. And I was scared, maybe, that I hadn't jumped out far enough; that I was going to hit a branch and crack my skull open; that I would land upside down in the water and drown. And when I hit the water I was really terrified, almost, it was like my brain froze up again like it had when Petrel nearly drowned. And then I was sinking down, down, much farther down than my knees, and this time the air was only inside me, and I felt a little clawing panic that maybe I didn't have enough, but I kicked my feet and then I was at the surface and I was laughing, laughing so hard I was almost choking, and my legs and arms felt numb and fluttery so that I had to float on my back because I didn't have enough strength to swim back to shore just yet.

When I got back, Petrel was waiting in the garden for me, wrapped in her blanket.

"Did you find it?" she asked.

"Yeah," I said. I was still laughing at the idea of it all, giddy that people could be afraid, that I could be afraid, of the air, of the sea, that anything familiar could turn so suddenly around. Maybe I should have been the Petrel, flying high and diving into the water, and she should have been the Sturgeon, hiding away from the world.

"Hmmph." She made an ugly little snort, but she sounded more like my sister, and I was feeling so light with relief at my own survival that I hugged her. She shuddered at the feel of my wet hair and salty skin, but she didn't scream.

Soon after that, I started sneaking salt into Petrel's food. When she wasn't looking, I would put a dash on her beets or sandwich. I'm not sure if she really didn't notice or if she just wanted to relearn to eat salty foods and was letting me poison her. Then she started eating eggs again, which was really the turning point. She ate only hard boiled chicken eggs at first, so well cooked that they almost had the texture of a rubber ball. Even though they were made in water the eggs themselves were totally solid and were therefore okay for her to eat. After a little while, she began to eat them scrambled.

You can sneak almost anything into a scrambled egg. Milk or water is the easiest and salt is a given. I cooked her eggs in butter, and then in vegetable oil, and then fish oil. I cooked them so stiff they were blackened on the bottom, and she never said anything. During the day, I would search the shore for gull's nests, stealing their eggs like a scavenger. I tried in vain to find turtle eggs, but I did find an unidentified bird's nest, hidden by the cliffs. I hoped it was a Petrel's nest. I pretended it was. *If anything would cure her, it would have to come from a Petrel*, I told myself. *If I am ever sick, I want to be fed on a diet of Sturgeons.* The idea made me a little queasy. It seemed almost cannibalistic.

I nursed her on sea bird eggs, ground up shellfish, and, as a last ditch effort, cooked a glass of sea water in with her breakfast. It smelled like low tide and had the consistency of thick gravy, and we both had diarrhea for a day and a half after we ate it.

But Petrel went back to school with me in the fall. We sat under our tree on the playground and I ate my lunch and she tried to hide the fact that she wasn't eating most of hers. She was pale from spending all summer hiding under a blanket, and I was tan from searching for birds nest and jumping out of trees. She was a little thinner than me. There was something funny around her eyes. There was no way around it: we looked different. Mother and Father never confused us anymore, and even teachers who barely paid attention or students who always used to keep their distance could call us by name. They knew us.

Actually, they knew Petrel; they only knew who I was by process of elimination. Suddenly, everyone was watching this skinny, dark haired girl with the circles under her eyes. The less skinny, somewhat healthier one was all but invisible out of context. Our classmates circled closer to us to eat their lunches. They talked to us after class and on the bus ride home. They wanted to know how Petrel was doing; they were very concerned. Was she feeling alright? Did she get enough sleep? They also suddenly valued her intellect. What did she think of that book we had to read for class last week? Did she think the math homework was very hard? And her favorites: favorite food, favorite author, favorite color. Suddenly, the whole class was eating hard boiled eggs for lunch and growing their hair out long. It made me nauseous. I had spent my life trying to differentiate between us, and here was a room full of copies.

At night, as the moon pulled the ocean closer to the shore, I jumped off cliffs and out of trees into its arms, trying to catch my breath again. I fell father and harder; landed deeper and wetter, but I never got hurt. And I never found that feeling again, no matter how cold the water or how dark the night. I would climb back in through the bedroom window soaking wet, and Petrel would be awake, waiting for me. I left little damp footprints on the comforter and the floor and she would tell me "You reek of the sea," and shut the window no matter how warm the air.

My hair would always smell like seaweed, and it made Petrel gag. She stayed away from me at school, and so the other children stayed away. It wasn't that she left me for her new friends, exactly. She wasn't interested in people anymore, at least not the way they were interested in her. They followed her around but she ignored them. She moved to a different tree to eat her lunch, and they followed her, sitting a slight distance away, but still closer to her than to me. She didn't talk to them unless they asked her a question, and it wasn't really talking in the way of conversation. She was monosyllabic or else spoke in a way they didn't understand; about the powers of the ocean and all the reasons she couldn't eat much salt. No one was eating much salt except for me.

One day they heard her call me "Stee," but someone thought she said "Steve," and thus the nickname began.

"Sturgeon Steve," Hilly Goose would ask me, "What is your sister bringing for lunch tomorrow? What is her favorite dessert? I want to bring some to share." Hilly Goose had a funny name too, but no one ever taunted her.

"Sturgeon Steve, Sturgeon Steve," We were too old for playground teasing, but that's what they did. They circled around me and threw breadcrumbs, of all things. They clung to my hair and got inside my clothes and made me itch. When I got home I ran straight into the water, clothes and all, even though Petrel screamed at me to stop.

"Stee! Stee!" she cried, pacing back and forth at the water's edge like a nervous canine, "Stop! Get out! Stop!"

When I got out I was crying.

"You stop," I told her. "Stop avoiding me. Stop letting them torture me!"

"I don't let them," she said, "They do whatever they want."

"They do whatever you want," I told her, "Or whatever they think you want. If you told them to stop, they'd stop."

"Wash your hair," she said, "And I'll come eat lunch with you again."

I cried and cried, but I washed my hair and didn't go swimming that night. Petrel sat on my bed and combed out all the tangles.

"Remember when you cut my hair?" I asked her.

"Remember when you cut my hair?" she said.

When she was done, she pulled a big tangle out of the comb and batted it around like a cat. She giggled maniacally until she couldn't breathe anymore and had to lay down on the throw rug.

"I love you Stee," she said. She'd never told me she loved me before. It was like she knew what was to come.

We finished seventh grade. We ate lunch under our tree. I washed the salt out of my hair or tied it up when I went swimming. The other children still called me Stevie or Sturgeon Steve, but it was easier to ignore when Petrel was ignoring them by my side. There were no more bread crumbs. There was no more fear.

We didn't see the other children much in the summer, because summer was a busy time for us. There was the garden to be tended, fish to catch and scale and salt, houses and boats to be re-weather proofed. And there were the summer storms of course: big dangerous monsters that made the winter blizzards look like sissies. These were storms with big hungry mouths that ate up everything in their path; sometimes spitting out bones of unfortunate boats or animals, but mostly keeping everything for itself. The sky could be sunny one second and the next would have clouds racing each other across the sky, spitting cold rain in a brief warning to those down below. It's a wonder any gardens survived.

Petrel and I were out on the sands when it happened. The sands were a long walk from home, but worth it for the white beach and clear water. In the middle of cliffs that went on for miles there was a cove where the tide went our farther than anywhere else, exposing what felt like miles of postcard perfect beach. If tourists ever came to our little town, this is the picture they would have sent home to their friends.

On a good day we could even dig for clams. If there was anything we loved, it was the sweet little salt water mollusks, and now that Petrel had returned to eating seafood she couldn't get enough of them. She was like a pregnant woman, hungry for the sea.

We had walked around the bottom of the cliffs instead of over them. It was harder going but ultimately faster because you didn't have the slow and careful climb and descent of the cliff sides. We had left at high tide in order to be at the sands before the turn, which meant we had walked a good deal in the water and were soaking wet. But the thought of clams moved us on. We were filling our buckets quickly but without any real sense of urgency, because it was early afternoon and we could always climb over the cliffs if it got too dark to walk home through the water, snapping open quahogs and eating them right there on the sand, squishing the raw bodies in our teeth as we dug for more.

Petrel had her back to the sea when the wave came. She was squatting in the sun, raking our trowel through the wet sand. We were too far out, of course, but you had to be too far out in order to get to get the clams. The tide went out so far and stayed out for so long that the sand in closer to shore was dry and any clams burrowed deep down in their clam hideouts. We had walked out far along the flat beach to where the sand turned into a fine mud, and the clams breathed little air bubbles up through the silt. Petrel was following the bubble trail of a runaway mollusk and never even saw it.

But I did. I was closer to the dry beach and heard a roar—a roar out of rhythm with the regular swishing waves and looked up just as an enormous wall of water caught my sister by the shoulders and ate her whole.

I was shouting for her, screaming for her, when the wave reached me. It took me by the ankles and knocked me down, dragged me on my back out of the cove. When I finally resurfaced the sky was darkening and those needle cold raindrops were slicing the water all around me. I couldn't see Petrel anywhere. I called for her and dove for her for what felt like hours, as my body numbed and my vision clouded with panic and the sky grew blacker and blacker.

There was a great crack of lightening and I saw her. She was further out than me, still in the choppy water.

"Petrel!" I screamed. I might have screamed my own name too. I swam towards her with frantic splashes, but she seemed to be getting farther and farther away with each bright flash, and it didn't look like she was swimming. Finally I realized I wasn't going to be able to reach her if all I was doing was dog paddling. I was the daughter of a fisherman and a Viking warrior, and swimming was in my genes. My blood was not pumped around in my veins—it swam. I took a deep breath. I took another. I tried to let my breath warm me from my frozen fear, discovered at last, discovered too late. I closed my eyes; I opened them and squinted through the rain. When the lightening blazed again, I crawled. I pulled my arms and kicked my legs harder than any Olympic Swimmer ever has. My body screamed for oxygen and I realized I had forgotten to breathe—and then I was there.

My sister was face down in the water, and her hair floated above her like seaweed. I flipped her over on her back, and tried to squeeze some air into her, but there was nothing I could do. The lightening was fading and I couldn't even tell which direction the shore was. I floated on my back and held her there on top of me until the storm passed and the evening sun began to peek through. The storm had pushed us back towards the beach, and once I got my bearings I began to swim us towards shore. Her body was cold. I thought mine was even colder.

I have never feared the ocean like my sister. When the sea is described as "fearsome," I cannot understand. Sometimes I think it was I who was taken under the waters that day, and it is I who will never return.

After the sea took Petrel for the third and final time, I had a dream. It wasn't a dream like the kind you hear others talk about after the death of a loved one, a sublime and blurry setting where the smiling deceased appears and says "It's going to be okay" and that they are at peace. In my dream I was on the beach by our house. I was standing, as instructed, in water up to my knees. I tried to walk out further but there was something blocking my path. I reached down to touch it and my hand slid into the water like oil.

The sea was slippery, and I could feel the grains of salt rubbing up against my fingers, like sand but sharper. My hand made a ripple, and the ripple began to spread out from me—further and further until I stood in a giant nebula of concentric rings. And then they froze. The ice spread out from where I stood, faster even than the ripples had, and I was trapped, knees and one hand stolen by the oily monster who had taken my sister.

In real life, no matter how cold it got, the beach never really froze. The ponds and rivers and any container of liquid left outdoors for a few hours turned into blocks solid enough to hold the truck. But the ocean remained wild and unchanged, as if the waves were too strong for the coldest weather to tame.

The dream scared me. It seemed I was frozen over too; that thrill seeking, freezing cold part of my brain had become solid when Petrel was finally gone. I feared it would never thaw.

That was the last time I dreamed.

Mother wanted to do a burial at sea. She didn't say so, but I imagined she would have liked to build a canoe and set it on fire once Petrel was inside. Vikings didn't fear the sea either.

But Father and I dissuaded her; I was positive Petrel would not want her final resting place in such an unstable, hungry, salty environment. So we buried her under the house, close to us. Mother wrapped her in her bedspread, and together we slid her into the narrow hole that Father had tunneled.

After the dirt was packed over her, I went inside and looked in the mirror. There was just me, and more me reflected back. The scene looked lopsided, and I realized I was standing in my customary spot on the right side of the sink. I moved to the middle and touched the glass. The girl in the mirror reached out too.

"Hey," I said, but she only moved her mouth in silence.

I didn't sleep that night. I sat on my bed, and I stared at her naked one. Mother had taken the quilt; I had stripped the sheets. In the dark I pulled up the mattress, blocked the window with its bulk. Maybe my sister had secrets she could keep from even me. Maybe the sea let her leave something behind.

I lifted the box spring and things began to fall out. Shells and sand. Feathers, crab legs and periwinkles, their owners long gone from this world. And there was my hair. Matted and tangled around the debris, it looked like fur. All together it looked like the bones of some wild animal, uncovered only by a coincidence of wind and time.

I realized I had its twin under my own mattress, and pulled out the sock of hair, the remains of the chocolate flower, and some other items I had stored under there over the years. They were not exactly the same, but they were not that different. I wrapped them all up, both sister's remains, and pushed them under the porch as well. Then I sat in the garden and watched the moon rise over the ocean, as if I was waiting for her to come home.

After Petrel was gone, I thought I was afraid of the sea. I wouldn't go
near it, wouldn't help Father on his boat, wouldn't cliff dive, wouldn't
even walk to the shore. I still ate fish, because I loved fish, and I
couldn't help it. Out of loyalty to my sister I ate more bread and
vegetables than usual. I showered more, washing and combing my hair
daily. I stayed away from the woods and cowered in my bed whenever
it stormed.

At school, the other children were finally nice to me. They offered
me bits of their lunches, sat with me on the bus ride home. They
chattered at me a little too brightly, coddled me a little too hard. But
they let me copy their answers when I caught sight of my reflection in
the window glass and became too shaken to think, and I passed eighth
grade by the skin of my teeth.

In the summer, I tended Mother's garden. I weeded and harvested
and became an expert at making tomato sauce and canning spicy
pickled green beans. Sometimes, when I dug too far down, I pulled up
clumps of hair. I pictured Petrel, buried beneath the house, her body
decaying but her hair still growing, even faster than mine. Or I pictured
her like a cat, burying hairballs years ago for me to dig up. They were
fossils; relics of another age where I was more than half a person.

Without Petrel, I became quiet. There was no one to fight with,
physically or verbally. Mother won any dispute without question, and
Father was too mild mannered to argue back. The kids at school agreed
with me too sweetly, too readily. They thought it would upset me if
they disagreed. They didn't call me Stevie anymore, or even Sturgeon.
Instead, they mysteriously began to call me Sally.

Who was this Sally? I wondered. Was she a third sister, or was I someone new? Could I become someone else if I tried? In ninth grade, my last year at the town school, I tried to be Sally. I pretended I fit in with the others. I sat with them at lunch at the newly installed picnic tables. I talked to the girls about the boys they liked. We compared stories of our father's fishing boats. We sat together on the bus, and I giggled like they did, but even my own laughter sounded fake to me. No one ever spoke of Petrel. It was like my entire twin-confused childhood had been erased. There had never been another identical girl to mix me up with. There had never even been a Sturgeon, only this Sally, who was secretly lonely in a way the old Petrel had never considered. The only evidence that there had been a double of me came when the other children swapped stories of our younger years, and sometimes I appeared in them doing something I was positive had happened to Petrel. But I didn't correct them. And maybe they really had forgotten her. Maybe they weren't doing it on purpose as some sort of cold comfort.

Mother wouldn't call me Sally. I didn't ask her too, didn't tell my family about my new persona. The truth was I knew I would never be a Sally. I was the big ugly fish, tied to the water, sister of the bird, now tied to the land. And the truth was, I didn't really want to be a Sally. Even with all its strange and bad memories, I loved our little house even more now that Petrel was underneath it. I loved its splintered driftwood stairs with the peeling paint. I loved the weathered shingles and the big gnarly tree that stood just outside the entrance, seemingly impervious to storms and age.

"I will never leave you," I told Petrel's box spring treasures. I added to her stash; little pebbles from the walkway, a red leaf, a pressed flower. Delicate things, things I imagined the fragile version of Petrel would have liked. I forgot about the times she hit me with icicles and

64

threw rocks at my head, or the time she held me down in a patch of spiky grass that gave me cuts all along my legs. The Petrel of my imagination was innocent and pure; a demure little angel who was too weak to go out, sitting on her bed and watching out the window with longing as I played on the shore. In my fantasy, I was a wonderful sister. I brought her presents from my journeys and spoke in poetic language of the things I had seen and the people I had met. I was charming and generous to a fault. I brought her her homework when she was too ill to go to school. I patiently went over class notes. I ignored my many invitations from my understanding friends to sit at the bedside of my invalid sister, feeding her spoonfuls of broth and reading her stories. I did not sneak extra salt that she hated in her food. I did not climb through the window in the middle of the night and drip water all over her blankets. We were so perfect and sweet that Mother never had to use her Viking stare, and Father spent blissful days fishing prosperously, and we ate his bounty without complaining.

We were a perfectly perfect family. When Petrel at last succumbed to her noble ailments, I held her hand as she whispered sweet parting words of inspiration to each of us. Her dark hair splayed out on the white pillow and tears rolled softly down my face. We buried her in an elegantly simple wooden coffin underneath the house because her last wish was that she could stay near us always.

When I went to the inland school in the fall, this was the story I took with me. My old schoolmates accommodating pity and suffocating niceness worked to my advantage; none of them corrected my past. I set myself up as a tragic heroine with amazingly poetic life, which allowed me to remain distant and aloof but not shunned. I didn't want to be Sturgeon Steve ever again. I tried not to remember that I ever was.

65

And then I met Pete.

We met in woodworking class, where I was trying to build a boat for my father. Specifically, I was trying to build an exact replica of his fishing boat, but as I hadn't been in or even near the real one in years, I was having trouble remembering most of the details, and I had to keep sanding out my carvings. The boat was getting smaller every day.

At the back of the woodshop was an enormous garage style door which could be opened in warmer weather. Today was one of those days left over from summer, and I was sitting just outside the door with my back leaning against the side of the building, halfheartedly sanding, eyes closed to dozing slits in the sunlight. I was trying to picture my father's boat, but only succeeding with a mental image of the apple tree behind the house with its almost ripe fruit. I really wanted an apple. I liked them sour. I would pick one when I got home, I decided, and imagined the tartness of the flesh beneath the tough skin. I could taste it.

Pete crouched down next to me, looked at the carving in my hands, grown still as I dreamt of apples. His hair was cut so short and so badly that he looked like a war victim. Scabs of scalp showed through little tufts of bristle.

"Would you like to go swimming with me?" he asked.

I told him no, absolutely not, I do not swim and I do not like the water. He had startled me so badly that I didn't wonder why he was talking to me. I had been at the school over a year, and once the celebrity story belonging to my pious and invalid sister had died down, my peers had lost interest in me, and I faded into the distance again. I had almost stayed at home rather than complete a second year, but at home I was treated exactly the opposite; I was too visible. My parents worried over my every move; Mother alternated between doting on me and shouting at me to do my chores and help her around the house and Father quietly caught me crabs and shrimp, my favorites, and didn't scold me for eating so many early apples. They were always there, hovering around me. It was like living in a hive of bees. We didn't mention Petrel, only cried occasionally when we thought we were alone.

So I went back to school in the fall, because being invisible was better. I was used to being alone, so alone my head would throb with it and I would reach out in the night for that missing piece, waking up freezing cold with that familiar ice pick in my brain. Maybe, I thought, if I distracted myself with my chores and with actually doing my schoolwork, my mind would be too busy to freeze up and I could sleep through the night again. It just turned out that the right distraction for me wasn't woodworking or math, it was Pete.

Because when he took off his sunglasses outside that day and looked at me, I agreed to go swimming before I could even think. When Pete looked into my eyes, I saw myself reflecting back. It was familiar, like something half remembered from childhood, and it gave me déjà vu, gave me vertigo. He brought back that danger feeling of falling, that itch to find the fear that other people felt all the time, and my adrenaline soared for the first time in over a year. And he smiled this smile, a little wistful, like he'd already known that I would agree.

He wanted to go swimming in the ocean, but I would not budge. The river passed near the back of the school, and I agreed to meet him there. I rode my bike, which my parents had bought for me after I missed the bus from school one too many times and had to take a two hour walk back home, nearly getting hit by a different bus. The thought was that I would be marginally safer with thin rubber tires separating me from the asphalt. I brought sour apples that Pete ate without comment, and then he waded in, fully clothed. I watched him do the backstroke without speaking, until he finally said, "Come on Sturgeon," and took me by the hand and dragged me in.

The feeling of the water was wonderful. The river wasn't as cold or as alive as the ocean, but I floated in it nonetheless. The summer had been dry, and the water was strangely warm. Weeds and dead leaves bumped against my legs. I imagined I was swimming in fish stew. I opened my mouth and as I sank the water slipped over my tongue. It tasted like dirt, like earth, like a grave. I came up sputtering, with Pete's hand wrapped around my arm.

"You almost drowned," he said.

"No I didn't." I told him, but for a moment I was confused. Had I almost drowned? How far down had I sunk? I had no memory of him pulling me out. It was the same old *Who am I?* vertigo of my misplaced youth.

"You know how to swim," he said. It was not a question. "So why don't you?"

I assumed he meant in the ocean, and I lied and told him I was afraid of the water, of the bottomless ocean, afraid of drowning and my body never being found.

He looked at me from under his peeling scalp.

"I know you," he said, "You're not afraid of anything." And I looked back at him, really looked at him this time, right down into those eyes that felt like falling, and I was afraid.

"Come on," he said, "let's float," and he twined his fingers in mine, so we were connected like tree roots and I had no hope of escaping, and we lay on our backs in the muddy water and watched the afternoon sun.

As soon as I left him and got on my bike, I forgot that I had ever been afraid. By the time I reached home, I needed to see him again. It was a physical pull, an adrenaline addiction as strong jumping off a twenty foot tree into the water. My body ached and my head throbbed for that need to feel weightless and dizzy again. So I snuck out, and went back to my tree, and somehow Pete was already there. We climbed up into the night and it felt like the bark and my hands stuck together and nothing bad could ever happen.

Then he pushed me.

He said afterwards that no, that wasn't how it happened, instead I'd slipped and that hand on my leg was him trying to catch me, not hurt me. But I'd climbed that tree a hundred times and never once come close to falling.

Luckily, we were near the top and I was on the water side, and I fell right out over the waves. I didn't have time to be afraid even, I felt literally petrified; my body had turned to wood, or ice, and the water was an unyielding solid surface. I thought about my dream and one hand hit the water first, twisting my wrist but breaking my fall for the rest of me.

The salt stung my skin as though it was scraped or burned. I opened my eyes but of course it was night and everything was black. For a second I couldn't tell which way was up, and then gravity took over and I bobbed back up to the surface, coughing. My wrist was on fire. I splashed around in a circle, trying to get my bearings, and then there was Pete again, hooking one arm around my torso and swimming me back towards shore, telling my all the while it was going to be okay.

He dragged me on the beach even though I struggled against him, pushed on my chest and told me to breathe.

"I'm breathing," I tried to say, but he put his mouth on mind and breathed into my lungs. His breath was strange and tasteless, and after a moment what we were doing felt less like CPR and more like kissing and so I sat up.

"I saved you," he whispered into my ear, into the night, into the ocean. "You would have drowned if it hadn't been for me."

"I'm fine." I said. "I don't need you."

"You should get home. Get out of those wet clothes." His eyes were like shark eyes. He wanted to undress my skin from my bones and swallow me whole.

"I guess I should," I said, even though he was the one shivering. I felt fine. Better than I had in years.

So I climbed back through my bedroom window, soaking wet and stiff with salt, and I expected to find Petrel there, holding a towel and full of resentment.

But she wasn't. There was nothing but an empty box spring, as hollow as I was.

Pete began to grow his hair out, and he liked me to scratch and rub his head; he said it itched as it came in. The sensation of his scalp under my fingernails was creepy, like running them along a chalkboard where pieces of the board flaked off and caught in my hands. I scratched harder and he purred like a kitten and pieces of his DNA curled up next to my skin.

I started meeting him every night; sneaking out my window just like old times. Pete would wait for me on the beach and we'd climb a new tree. Or we'd hike the other way until we got to the cliff face and go up until our hands bled and the salt stung our palms. Once we swam out so far we hit a sand bar and walked along it in water just above our shins to where the rocks rose like gunnels in the night, soundless but for the gentle shift of the waves. We climbed to the top of the flattest one, and I felt I could stay there forever, stretched out with Pete's hand in mine, watching the moon and breathing in the clean salt air, heart pounding with the danger of the approaching tide and the dreadful familiarity beside me.

I stopped sleeping at night. I barely stayed awake during my classes, falling into a hypnotic half-conscious state where I felt always in danger of slipping out of my chair. I began to crave the sensation of falling more and more. If my heart was not rushing, I was not really alive. I forgot about the false Petrel the same way I forgot about the real one. I forgot about my family and my chores, about eating and drinking and homework. Teachers kept passing me; my tragic history still afforded me just enough leeway to get sympathy marks, but I wasn't learning; I was barely even present.

I grew thinner, and paler. My bones jutted out at weird angles. The circles under my eyes were dark as bruises. I began to get a phantom ache around my ribcage and my left wrist. When I looked in the mirror I didn't see anyone. Not Petrel, not Sturgeon—no one. It was just the blank face of a stranger; someone you might see looking out from the pages of a magazine ad. With all the not-eating, I got dizzy a lot, which I liked, because dizziness felt like vertigo which felt like falling which was the only thing keeping the blood pumping in circles around my body. I would sit there in delight, watching math equations swim across the board, dark orbs flickering on the edge of my vision.

Pete insisted that I take him home to meet my family, so one night we sat across from Mother and Father at our old oak table, and Pete dropped his hand from mine so he could grab onto his bowl of fish stew with both hands. He held it close to his body like someone was going to steal it from him, eating quickly and soundlessly, using Mother's thick peasant bread to soak up every last piece of peppercorn, each wayward scale.

Mother refused to look at him; she sat stonily at the table shredding her bread into her bowl but not eating it, getting up abruptly and leaving the room. Even my gentle father could barely summon a word. His eyes were watery and disappointed, and looked only at me. I sat there cradling my hand, the one with the aching wrist that Pete was holding earlier, feeling somehow rejected for my parent's fish stew.

Afterwards we walked down to the beach. Pete tried to take my hand back but I wouldn't let him. He thanked me for dinner with such enthusiasm that I couldn't even be bothered to tell him that he had been the only one eating. The wind had picked up, and he asked to see my father's boat. I told him it was moored out too far for even us to swim to.

"Let's take the dinghy," he said, and began to untie it before I had a chance to agree. Was I going to agree? I wasn't sure, but I felt like I already had, and I didn't have the strength anymore to argue.

We squeezed together on the middle seat and each took an oar, stroking together until we reached the boat. It was a sturdy but small fishing boat, equipped to catch whatever was in season. The wooden deck was smooth and worn down with my father's feet, the side rails polished with his weather resistant gloves.

Pete scrambled aboard, the rocking dinghy floating me from side to side, increasing my vertigo. I tied it off and followed him on board.

"Look at the moon, Stee," he said, and his voice was high and breathy. The wind was blowing even more now, and it played pieces of his hair out from its ponytail. I turned to look at the moon and my own hair tore free, and that was when something began to awaken inside me. Some deep dread began to grow out of all the stories and the lies and the haze of near starvation.

"What did you call me?" I asked. I had to should over the sound of the wind. Maybe I had heard him wrong.

He just laughed and held his arms up to the moon, while clouds crawled over it like ants.

"Pete!" I yelled, and he turned to look at me, and I didn't know whose eyes I was meeting.

He took my shoulders and pushed me, and I fell, hitting the back of my head losing my footing.

"What do you want from me?" I asked, or thought, or thought I asked. The rain had started and it was hard to tell what things were.

His face leaned down above me and there were the eyes; fierce, angry eyes. They were her eyes, and my eyes, and the eyes of someone else I never wanted to know.

He kissed me on the mouth, and his lips were neither hot nor cold, just wet with the rain and the slick oily ocean. He kissed me and I struggled away and then he hit me in the side of the head, hard, with the bony heel of his hand. My ear began to ring and I grabbed at Pete but my balance was off and I only got his hair, and then I was pulling at him and pushing and screaming angry, unintelligible words because I knew if I stopped for a second, if I let myself go quiet and calm again, I would die.

And he had a knife suddenly, a big dangerous looking thing that maybe my father used to cut nets that were tangled. He swiped in at my hand that was locked in his hair but I didn't move even when he cut me—couldn't move in fact, I was holding onto it like it was the only thing keeping me grounded in the storm. Then he was sawing through the hair I held, and then he was sawing through the line that held the

73

dinghy, and then he hit me again with the handle of the knife and the last thing I saw through the haze of storm and lost consciousness was a lithe form with wild hair leaping for the dinghy. And really, it could have been anyone.

When I woke up, it was morning and my head was throbbing. I touched the puffed up skin on the side of my face and it was swollen and sunburned and covered with a thick layer of salt. The sun was so bright I could only open my eyes in quick blinks. The waves were calm and blue and gentle, barely waves at all, and my left hand was coiled so tight in something it was almost white with bloodlessness. I sat up to unwrap it and my head felt light—lighter than lightheadedness, lighter than vertigo and low blood sugar. My hair was cut off roughly around my ears. But did it match the chunk wrapped around my hand? I unwound it and the blood rushing into my hand stung, but I couldn't tell whose hair it was, and my head hurt so badly I wasn't sure if it was hair at all. I let it go over the side and it fell straight down, and I could watch it sink.

There was a sharpness to the air that wasn't usually present after a big storm. I lay back down in the bottom of the boat and watched the streamlined white clouds speed across the sky. The wind was cold, like the wind from early fall. I imagined I had been floating here for months. I had missed summer as I turned into a piece of broken driftwood. I could be anywhere. I could even have floated around the world and ended up exactly where I had started.

I sat up. I saw the familiar coastline; the trees I had leapt out off, the cove where Petrel had been taken. There was our little beach, and in the distance I thought I could maybe see the top of the sentinel tree outside our door. My father's boat was waterlogged but had somehow held its mooring. The dinghy, of course, was gone. My head throbbed, and my hair was stuck to my forehead with some dried blood the storm hadn't managed to wash away. My clothes were stiff with salt and cold with the sea and I searched around the little cabin until I found a big old sweater of my father's which had escaped the rain. I took off my shirt and used it to wash the rest of the blood off my face and put on the sweater instead. It smelled like my father smelled when he had just come home from fishing; like fresh seaweed and fishy bait and the ripe smell of low tide. I had a sudden longing for home.

I sat all day on the boat, the boat which had once been named after Petrel and I, but which had had its name scratched off after her death. My father loved his boat, but not as much as he loved us, and he had never bothered to rename it. I thought about repainting it for him, of scraping and sanding and the smell of turpentine, of the satisfaction of hard labor and building something from nothing. I would name it something new, maybe my mother's name. My mother wasn't going anywhere. The idea of manual labor appealed to me. I could quit school for real, work my father's boat the way I hadn't been able to when I was a child. I would rise at dawn, sleep at dusk, purge the sea of its most shrewd and hidden fish. My muscles would become hard knots of steel wire, and I would be able to take on anything. I drifted off to sleep.

I awoke and the sky was orange. My legs were stiff and aching, my fingertips spotted white, and I couldn't even feel my feet. I took off my boots and wrung out my socks, pulled up my knees and stretched the sweater down over them so I could tuck my feet underneath. I wrapped a tarp around me and watched as the sun finished its descent. I was too numb to feel the wind, or maybe it couldn't touch me anymore. Maybe I was above all of it, or below, underwater somehow, looking up at

75

myself.

I could have gone into the more sheltered cabin but felt unable to move. I was calm for the first time in what seemed like my whole life; a real calm that reached all the way down to my Viking bones. I had no desire to jump off any trees, or befriend terrifying strangers, or pull my sister's hair. I wanted nothing more than to sit on this deck forever as the light grew dimmer all around me. No one else in the world existed. The wind died down, and the waves lapped softly against the sides of the boat. Stars began to blink out in the darkness, like they were sending me a message in Morse code.

I was a lone sailor lost at sea, and they were trying to lure me home.

The Mirror

Once upon a time, as the stories go, there was a glass in a wood. It was wrinkled and rippled with age, green and brown around the edges, and pockmarked with mildew. Birds came to gaze at themselves, always on Tuesday. Though what sense of the days of the week do birds have? Do they tick by in the forest the same way if there is no calendar to mark them? Do the birds know a Tuesday is a Tuesday is a Tuesday, or do they only know by the mark of the sun upon their beaks?

They only know there is a glass. They are pulled to it like a magnetic North every seventh day at dawn.

Lucas was the only blond person she had ever met. He had pale thin hair that he kept cut short, and it stuck straight up in places like spikes. In the summer months she tried to flatten it out for him, but when winter came he wore a red cap, which Papa didn't like of course, because it showed up in the snow.

She and Papa were dark as ashes, and the others were varying shades of brown, but all had faces pale enough to glow in the moonlight. Papa said it was to help them hide in the snow, though who they were hiding from he never said. An always assumed it was another of his fairy tales.

Papa loved stories. He told her Russian tales of foolish princes and beautiful girls, and scary stories with morals from Germany, where he used to live. When An was little she used to shriek at his witches' voices and laugh at his animal sounds; Lucas and the other men smiling or grimacing in the background. Every night there was a new tale, and Papa never seemed to run out.

Once, there was a girl. She was young, but not as young as she should have been. She lived with her father and mother in a great big house, a house far too big for three little people. They had once been rich (but now they weren't), and when it was winter (as it was now), the house was very cold. The walls were stone, stone older than the girl and older even than the father (who had lately been getting gray around the edges), and the heat fell away from them like leaves.

The mother and father, who missed their old lifestyle, pinned all their hopes of redemption on the girl. They sold their wedding china and their jewelry, their first edition books and paintings, but left everything in the girl's room untouched. She was their hope, their dream, their way out, and their aspiration crushed her with its' unyielding weight until she thought her lungs would stop.

If Papa had his way they would all wear shades of white and gray, with hints of brown and maybe black for night. They would travel forever, plodding through snowdrifts and driving on icy, uncleared roads, never stopping, even at night, taking shifts to sleep and eat and warm and chill.

But Papa stopped for her, because when she was small, Lucas told her, she had cried and wailed at the freezing winds and the glaring suns and the constant motion, and could not sleep through the night unless there was absolute stillness.

"An," Papa would say to wake her, and she liked the way it sounded, like the English word "on." Like he was saying "On, on!" every morning when it was time to go. Lucas knew a little English, and she was pretty sure Papa knew more than that, though he never spoke it when he knew she was listening.

"An," he was saying now, "are you ready to go? We still have a few hours left of daylight."

She nodded and stood, waiting for Lucas to follow her. He stretched and pulled his muscles forward and his hair, which she had carefully flattened, sprung up again.

"Are you cold?' she asked. Lucas was always cold, though he didn't like to admit it. "Do you want your hat?"

He shook his head. He had pale stubble on his cheeks, and it glowed in the afternoon light. His skin puckered with goose pimples. The cold was coming.

Once upon a time, I lived in a house, in a real house with walls and even half a roof and a real dirt floor I kept nice and clean, or as clean as a dirt floor can keep. In the summer it was wet and in the winter it was cold, but still it was my home and I could call it mine.

I was re-making the roof because the water would come down, straight down, drip drip drip onto my head in my bed, and even if I slept the other way round my feet got wet. So I was up there, fixing it, when there was crying and shouting and a stampede of brown legs and feet coming my way, and somebody, I didn't see who though I have my suspicions, pushed me, just knocked the ladder out from under me and I fell straight down, flat down, and I heard something snap and it wasn't my ladder.

One of my eyes went out; it just went out like a sundown. It didn't hurt any, it didn't feel like anything, nothing felt like anything, and I got scared for my eye, and for whatever had snapped and for whatever all those feet were running from. And I tried to get up and follow but nothing happened, not in my feet or in my legs or in my one eye. My arms twitched around a little and my hands felt fiery.

And then I saw what everybody was running from. Saw pale eyes and paler skin, pale clothes and pale hair, saw a ghost. These ghosts, they talked with pale words and they touched me; touched me all over my body and I couldn't feel a thing except for where my scream vibrated in my lungs.

And they picked me up and carried me, carried me away from my home and down the sand hill and put me in a boat on the water, but a bigger boat than I'd ever seen before, and I tried to tell them that my roof wasn't done and the water was going to leak into the bedcovers, but they just stared at me with their eyes like snakes like they didn't understand a word I said.

She was fourteen when Jessica came. Jessica touched everyone. She brushed An's hair, and she straightened Lucas's clothes, and she took Papa to bed and touched him everywhere until he glowed. They stopped more and more often, and some days they never went anywhere at all. Papa and Jessica stayed in the caravan all day, and An had to wait outside until they opened the door, which had never been locked to her before. At first she sat on the top step like always, but there were noises from inside and Lucas made her come away. They played games with the others, first with sticks and then later with cards and dice. She learned to tell when the men were lying and they learned she wasn't a child any more. Papa had abandoned her for this new touching thing, but that was all right. She had seven other friends who would never leave her.

They put me in a cage. A cage house with a cold shiny floor and dull and colorless walls. Twice a day a woman with skin the color of honey comes to feed me. I try to get her to talk to me, to tell me who these ghost men are, and why my arms and legs are frozen, but I can see it in her eyes how scared she is. She lifts my head and spoons gray goop into my mouth and she whispers a chant so low I cannot make out the words, but it sounds like a prayer.

She wears a little silver chain, with a symbol dangling down. It is two silver sticks overlapping like a wall frame. Sometimes it hits me in the side of the face, but I am so starved for physical contact I do not even mind this. I want to grab it and catch her and make her stay, but I cannot move my arms.

The effort makes water collect in my eyes like rain, and she sees it, and she prays louder. Mary, she whispers, Mary, Mary, Mary.

She points at me with the spoon, also silver, though duller and less careful.

Mary, she incants, and maybe this is just what they call me here, in this desolate cage. Maybe this is my name, my ghost name. Maybe it is a spell to keep me in the cage of my body.

Papa let his beard grow out and Jessica wore scarves wrapped around her chest instead of shirts in summer. Her full breasts never left Papa's eyes, and a muscle moved in his throat whenever she raised her arms. Her skin darkened in the sun.

When winter came, Jessica gave her a present, a little mirror, metal backed, with only a tiny crack to mar its shiny surface. It folded in half on silent hinges, small enough to fit inside a pocket. An was fascinated by her reflection, and the way she looked a little like Papa but also not at all like him. Jessica tried to curl An's hair to match her own, but it hung in fuzzy clumps around her face. She asked Lucas if he wanted to see what he looked like, but he did not. Jessica rode inside instead of walking in the snow.

Their most prized possession was the enormous gilded mirror that hung above the girl's bed. The frame swirled and swooped in gold and copper loops, and the glass itself was so unblemished that when the girl looked in it hardly seemed as though she was looking at anything other than real life.

When she moved her hand, a copy of her hand waved back. When she nodded her head, an identical chin bobbed in front of her. And when she closed her eyes, she saw nothing at all.

When they were finally caught, it was the glow of the fire that gave them away. Ten men rode up on horseback and surrounded them, guns at their hips as two dismounted. Jessica was in the caravan, and An dozed by the fire. Lucas grabbed her arm and pulled her tightly closer, and the shock of his sudden contact woke her fully. The mirror in her skirt pocket pressed at her hip.

"At last, we find you," said one of the men. He spoke Russian, but his accent was strange and his words were heavy. He looked at the men seated by what was left of the fire, eyes unsure where to rest.

He pointed at An with his gun and with his chin.

"What is your name?"

Lucas squeezed her arm tighter.

"Anuva." she stuttered, whispered, breathed.

"And who is your father?" he squinted his eyelids against the falling snow.

"I am." Lucas spoke, and Papa didn't move. The man with the gun stepped closer and pulled off Lucas' red cap. The hair beneath rose to attention.

"What is your name?" He threw the cap in Lucas' lap, but he didn't move.

"Luke," he said, meeting the man's gaze, not squinting at all.

The man said something in English that An couldn't understand. His beard was blond like Lucas'. Lucas answered back, and she saw her father's eyes widen. The man spat in the snow in front of them; a brown glob of tobacco rested by her toes.

"Dwarf," he said. He snarled like a dog. "Pitiful creature. When we find her, we will take her. If you are lying, we will kill you."

Look for me. Look for me here in this cage where the ghost-men come. I am laid out here on the floor, but I wouldn't know it. I can imagine a field of grass or my bed under the leaky roof. I try to feel the floor, but it's like it isn't there. It's like I'm floating, but I'm so heavy that I'm drowning. I can't move anything except my head, a few fingers, my throat. All my parts work fine, but I'm not controlling them. They work separate from me. I am a giant puppet. A child's toy.

When the ghost-men come, they come inside. I know what is happening. I can see them do it, but I cannot feel it. Sometimes I slide across the floor, and sometimes they grunt and make noises in their own language. Sometimes they pull my hair, and that I can feel.

Sometimes I am pregnant.

Sometimes I am not.

Sometimes, many times, but I do not know how long, a baby comes out. A ghost-man, or sometimes a ghost-woman, reaches a big white hand up inside me and pulls the babies down. These babies, they are half-ghost and half-me. They are ugly, and they are not mine, but they cry like me. They scream as loud as I do.

That night, An slept in the caravan with Papa and Jessica, but she couldn't get warm. She kept thinking about the man with the gun; his

83

squinted brow, the way he wiped the tobacco juice from his short beard with one glove. About the fire in his eyes when he looked at Lucas, and when he looked at her.

She put on her boots and her coat and opened the door quietly. Lucas and some of others were still outside; they had stoked the fire higher than usual, and were throwing things into it. She went and stood by Lucas, the snow melt under her boots making her feel unstable and wobbly, like a toddler.

Lucas didn't look at her, and she couldn't think of anything to say.

"I don't think you look like a dwarf," she said finally.

Lucas stopped moving, and the others did too. For a few moments, only their shadows moved, flickering softly in the light of the flames.

"Once upon a time," said Lucas, slowly shredding the paper he was holding and feeding it to the flames, "There was a beautiful woman who lived in a very cold place. She wished for a baby more than anything in the world. 'If I had a baby,' she would say, 'with skin as white as snow, hair as black as coal, and eyes as blue as ice, I would never be lonely again. I would love her, and hold her, and never let anyone harm her.' Nine months later, she gave birth to a beautiful little girl. With her dying breath, she named the child—"

"Snow White," said An, "I know this story."

When my body is tired, it feels like a house. Not my light, beautiful, airy house, but the house where I live now, the house around the cage. It feels heavy and full of water and cold. My feet and legs, which I haven't felt in a long long time, burn with this cold. I can't stop shivering. I have never been this cold before.

The ghost men, they bring me a piece of glass and show me my reflection. I have not seen it in so long, not since I was young and

84

happy and free, and my biggest worries were a leaky roof and day old bread.

I am frightened.

That is not me in the mirror. That woman in the mirror is pale and gray. Without the sun, she is almost as pale as the ghost men, and her hair is shock white and she has no teeth. Where did my beautiful teeth go?

This is a ghost, a colorless ghost.

"No," said Lucas, throwing the last of the shreds in front of him. "She named her Anuva. An old Russian name, a beautiful name. It means 'new beginning.'"

When it rains, the mirror's concave surface fills with a shallow pool, water so shiny you can almost make out the individual droplets separating and reforming their molecules into something brand new. The birds sip at it and chirp to each other, positive that this water tastes better than any other water; this water is the water they come back to drink again and again, and this is why.

"But that's my name," said An. She crossed her arms over her chest. She didn't remember Lucas ever telling her a story, even when she was very small.

I buck my head forward to smash the glass. They laugh at me. I move only the tiniest bit. I pound my head back on the cold cold floor instead.

"Once upon a time," said Lucas, still watching the fire, "there was a

85

very wicked man, who came from a place almost as cold. He had loved the beautiful woman, and it made him angry. He hated her black hair and he hated her name and he hated everything about her, but he loved her. And it made him so angry that he killed her. But first, he killed her mother. And then he killed her father. And then he killed her uncle, her brother, her cousins far and wide, cousins she had never met and never would. He killed people like her wherever he could find them.

"And when killing them no longer made him satisfied, he went back to the beautiful woman, and he killed her too.

"When he thought she was dead, he felt better. And he went away. And he thought he would be happy.

"But she wasn't dead yet. When the woman's husband came home, he found a baby bathed in blood, too much blood for a normal childbirth. And he found written on the floor 'Anuva,' a good name, a Russian name, a name without past or history. And he picked up the baby and he erased the writing and he ran, back to the old country, back to the snow. And he hasn't stopped running since."

"What was his name?" An asked, barely breathing. Her legs shook, and the mirror bounced against them.

"The father?" asked Lucas, and she nodded, a tiny nod.

"His name was Grisha. Also a Russian name. A name that means 'watchful,' a name with promise and caution and love for his daughter."

Lucas turned to meet her eyes. His pale beard glowed red in the firelight.

"It wasn't always Grisha. It used to be something else, something that must never be spoken or known. Something like Aaron or Samuel. Something secret."

She reached out to touch him, hesitantly, slowly. She cupped his

86

face in her palm, and his beard was scratchy and warm on her bare skin.

She wished she was small again, small enough to hide inside this warmth.

His eyes were sad, and tired. They stood the same height.

Sometimes, she was sure, the reflection changed. Sometimes she was looking at a young girl, pale, with eyes too big and cheeks too small, and sometimes there was a woman, still pale (but not sallow), still big eyed (but without dark circles underneath), and cheeks still thin but not sunken. She was beautiful, but strange. She wasn't like the robust, smiling women in the paintings that had once hung in the gallery room, or delicate like the winged fairies carved into the covers of some of her books. The woman in the mirror was homely and serious but she was also striking and gorgeous. She was the most fascinating person the girl had ever seen. She would have stared at her for hours, but the mirror always changed back to her own reflection.

"Eventually, the evil man must have gone back. He must have had second thoughts, or maybe he wanted to desecrate the beautiful woman, or burn her, or bury her. He must have seen her flattened belly, heard the silence of the absent baby, realize what had happened.

"And he began to search. Search for babies and fathers with Jewish names. Babies with long black hair and eyes like her mother's. Search for someone else, to love or to hate, to have or to hold."

"Mirror, mirror, on the wall," she would say, asking it questions she could not ask her parents, tiptoeing up and down the hallways of their silent tomb. It the dark of the night when all the reflections were

87

shadows she lit candles and stared at the surface, wondering who she really was.

"He had help, didn't he?" An asked. She didn't want to say his name.

Lucas nodded, the movement of his head sending his warm breath across her wrist.

"There were some who still loved him, who loved his daughter born in blood."

"Seven," she said, because it was a fairy tale number, and also because it was true.

He nodded again.

"Seven men, men who had also loved and lost, or who maybe had some blood on their own hands." His eyes flicked around to the faces at the fire. Not one turned away.

"And they—we—travelled. Deeper into the snow, farther from the evil man and his minions."

"But the father—he got lonely," An knew the rest. "He missed the beautiful woman, and he loved the daughter, and he loved the men, but it wasn't enough for him."

"And he took a lover," Lucas stepped closer to her. "A woman who reminded him of his murdered wife. A woman he could forget himself in."

"And he grew careless."

"And the caravan slowed."

"And the colors brightened."

"And the baby grew up, and she grew older, and taller, until there was simply not enough room for her."

"And she loved her friends, and she missed her father."

"And one day, the evil man caught up with them."

"And it was almost the end."

"But it wasn't, not quite yet."

Lucas touched her chin and she thought she would catch fire. He put his lips on hers for a brief moment that lasted an eternity, but it wasn't really a kiss, more like he was breathing into her, warming her with his breath, bringing her to life. The flames crackled and sparked behind them like they would consume the whole world.

When I die, I will haunt them. I will be in every mirror, I will be the ghost. I will scream and I will move, and I will reach through the glass and squeeze them til they break. I will be a spectre, a spirit, a phantom, a wraith. I will be gray and I will be white, and when I have found them all I will go away, I will leave be, and I will find my little house by the water and I will sink into it, full of colors.

I am tired. I am so, so tired. Tired of this life that is not a life, these children that are not children, these men who are not men.

Who am I now?

I am nothing.

I will be nothing.

Someday.

"How does the story end?" she asked, a little warmer.

Say my name. You know it. Say it three times in the dark. I die. Look for me.

"Look in the mirror," said Lucas. "She knows."

When there is no rain, the glass is dry and shiny, stretched taught in the

89

sun. The birds admire their warped reflections, and each time they look better than the last. Time passes, and they begin to believe they are as pretty as they look in the glass. Each feels mightier than the others, and dips its' beak scornfully to get another look.

It is beautiful.

Butterfly Weather

On Monday morning, there were ants in the kitchen. I searched under the sink in vain for the traps I knew I had bought. I tried the medicine cabinet, the hall closet, and finally found them on top of the refrigerator, out of my reach without the assistance of the step stool. I was twenty minutes late for work.

When I got home, there was a funeral procession on my window sill. Tiny black bodies marching in single file past the already full traps, swarming over my browning bananas and into the living room and behind the couch. I searched for hole in the screen but couldn't find anything. I threw away the traps and reluctantly got out the spray. I didn't like killing things, but this kitchen was my domain. I didn't go into their hills and eat their old fruit, and I expected the same courtesy out of them.

I spent my evening vacuuming up tiny carcasses, feeling a little sad. My apartment was now the site of a massacre. I put on The Beetles as a kind of eulogy, pushing the vacuum handle back and forth to the rhythms.

On Tuesday, it was ladybugs. My whitewashed walls looked polka dotted, like a crawling Jackson Pollock. I sealed my kitchen window with painter's tape and it was covered with the beetles almost immediately. If I blurred my eyes, I had a purple frame around a pleasant scene of the building across the street. I opened the door and tried to shoo them away, but they ignored me, preferring instead to recline on my couch and read my discarded magazines. I threw away the bananas the ants had decimated and took the garbage out. I left the windows open when I went to work, even though it was only February.

On Wednesday I woke, groggy and cranky, to a day overcast and dark. I hadn't slept well, imagining every second that I felt little red beetles crawling through my bedclothes. I got into the shower without the aid of my contacts, and when I emerged found that the sun was shining after all, I just couldn't see it through the mass of crickets covering the windows.

Hundreds, maybe thousands, of black bodies writhing and crawling, trying to get out or maybe just admire the view. I called an exterminator and fled.

After work I was hesitant to cook, so I stopped for take-out on the way home. Chicken lo mein and spring rolls in hand, I walked up the stairs to a deafening roar and a note on the door with a single word: "Sorry—" scribbled with a dying pen.

It was dusk and the crickets were singing. Not chirping forlornly on a hearth, or musically chattering as background noise on a camping trip, but mounting a full scale opera in the six hundred square feet I had formerly called home. I took my Chinese food to the car.

Nothing surprises you, my fortune cookie said, *You are ready for whatever comes your way.*

I awoke early Thursday morning with a terrific crick in my neck, just in time to see a black cloud rising from my kitchen window, swirling upwards and into the dawn. I turned on the car to check the time and listen to the news. It was 6:41, and there was nothing on the air about a bug invasion. I went upstairs, changed my sheets, called into work, and fell into a deep and quiet sleep.

I awoke later to a new sound and knew I was not alone. There was clicking and swishing coming from all corners of the room, almost like the hush of a distant ocean. I opened my eyes and my bedroom was a sea of iridescent green and gold, and my bed a still island in the midst of roiling waves. I spilled out of bed and jumped as far as I could, rushing and swimming to the hall closet. I ousted the vacuum and pulled the door shut behind me, but I could hear the tide of june bugs rustling closer. I found my gym bag and pulled on sneakers, shorts, a sports bra and a sweatshirt and bolted from my apartment, not even bothering to shut the door against the tidal wave within.

To my surprise, the invasion had spread and there was gold and green everywhere in the parking lot below. It seemed to be raining beetles, and I pulled my hood up against the spray. My bare legs goose-pimpled in the cold. How were the bugs alive in this weather? Weren't june bugs summer creatures?

I ran along Pine Street and took a right on Main, carapaces crunching beneath my feet like crunchy fall leaves. As I reached the one mile mark by the elementary school the swarm thinned, less of a blizzard and more of a drizzle. Little kids in their winter coats kicked bugs at each other and laughed on the playground, building castles in their june bug sand box. I found a couple dollars in my pocket and stopped at Mike's for a cup of coffee.

Inside, everyone was jumpy and skittish. Beetles swam in their lattes and played on the espresso machine. The barista tried to sweep them out with a broom, but more came in when he opened the door. I bought a bottle of water instead and continued my run.

Around Fourth Avenue the wind picked up and I was bombarded by tiny thick bodies, surprisingly heavy for their minute size. I squinted around their hairy legs and tried to keep going, deciding to cut my run short and head back.

At home the beetles had taken to the air, flying in dizzy circles, making laps around my living room. By three o'clock they were all dead, finally succumbed to the February chill. My vacuum, already choked with ant bodies, finally gave up and joined them. I spent the afternoon sweeping bug shaped jewels out onto the landing. All of my neighbors were doing the same thing. Our staircase glittered in the sunset.

On Friday, work called me to say not to bother coming in, the office was covered in Katydids. I already knew; I'd awoken to find my belongings blanketed with what looked like pale spring leaves. I had trees where there had once been lamps, bushes of footstools, and a small hill for a refrigerator. I was living in a crawling forest. Bugs as big as my palm were nesting in my hair. I found my phone under a new growth and rang my favorite Chinese take away, but their kitchen was alive and they were closed for the day.

I called a few friends to see if I could hide out at one of their places until the invasion was over, but they were equally green. Maurice had a newborn baby and was worried she would get lost under the swarm if she set her down for a second. She had spent the entire morning pacing her upstairs landing and shooing bugs off her daughter. I decided I was better off at home.

In the closet I found my camping gear; a tent, sleeping bag, tiny cookstove, and mattress pad. I set the tent up in the living room, taking several hundred lives in the process. Armed with my laptop, some books, leftover lo mein from Tuesday and a bottle of water, I hunkered down in my sleeping bag. Katydids crawled over the canvas, blocking the light and shaking the tent, which miraculously did not collapse. I was worried I would end up like Maurice's baby, smothered between cloth and this new living forest. I found some old power bars in the pocket of the tent and ate them as I waited.

On Saturday, it was quiet. I awoke in the predawn light to an absence of sound and movement. It was unnerving. I emerged from the tent expecting to find piles of dead green bodies, but there was nothing. I checked the rest of my apartment, but everything, including the kitchen window, was silent and still. I hesitantly tried my bed, and, finding it free of six legged friends, climbed in. Outside my window it was snowing.

I awoke energized, alone. I used my kitchen for the first time in days to make real hot food; coffee, a bagel, some fried eggs and bacon. Afterwards, feeling overstuffed, I decided to go for a run. I dressed warmer this time, and brought my own water.

Outside the snow continued to fall, not piling up on the ground but blowing and drifting. The sun was shining and the air was crisp, and I realized what I thought were snowflakes were actually tiny white butterflies riding the air currents and resting on immobile objects. The light shone through their translucent wings and sparkled in the morning sun. The effect was kind of beautiful, though I was glad they were not in my apartment.

As the day went on and the temperature gradually rose the butterflies grew bigger and more colorful. At noon they were yellow and pale orange and the size of my fist, and the sunset that night was eclipsed by enormous winged insects, some prehistoric in size and all vibrant shades of red, orange, and purple.

It seemed the whole city was outside, enjoying this latest infestation. People fired up their grills and got out their lawn chairs. It felt like the Fourth of July with a butterfly fireworks show.

As dusk fell, smaller butterflies emerged in muted blues and grays.

95

They swirled around us in great clouds, tasting hamburgers and lighting on bacci balls, picking up their more colorful companions and flying up, up, and away, until all that was left was the darkness and the wondering voices of my neighbors, so near in the fallen light.

On Sunday the bugs were gone. I waited impatiently until mid-afternoon to see who the latest arrival would be, only to find my apartment still quiet and alone. I walked to Mike's for the sheer sake of having something to do, and bought a coffee and a newspaper.

"Butterfly Weather?" The headline questioned, as though it wasn't sure it had all happened either. It was the top story, quoting various local scientists and politicians, who, in more words than the front page, admitted they didn't know either. Beside the story was the black and white photo of a young girl, taken midmorning judging by the size of the insects, holding mittened hands up, tongue out, trying to catch a butterfly snowflake any way she could.

I finished my coffee slowly, thinking how quiet it was with only the hum of people. I leafed through the paper, but there was no mention of insects in any of the world or national news. I left the barista a generous tip, recognizing him as the one who had to sweep up all those bodies during what seemed like another lifetime ago. Outside the sun was shining, unobstructed. I cleared my dishes, put on my coat, and walked back to my empty apartment.

Knees Together

When I got on the train that night, I knew it was over. I knew this was the last time I would be riding with him, and I knew that this time we wouldn't chicken out from the cold and the uncomfortable plastic seats, but we would stay buried beneath the city all night long, only emerging from our metal beds in time to see the last sunrise.

Asher got there first, because he is perfect.

"Hey," I said.

"Hey yourself." He handed me a token. "I bought you a token." I rolled its smooth metal edges between my fingers.

Because it was our last time, I did not say "I can afford it myself, thanks," and I did not say "I don't need your charity," and I did not say "Let me pay you back."

"Thanks," I said.

We pushed the coins into the slots and the doors slid open.

"Back or front?" asked Asher.

"Middle," I said, just to be obstinate.

We sat down on the hard white plastic. No one was sitting across from us, so we stretched our legs out as far as they would go. We both still wore Doc Martins, but his were cleaner. He put his arm around my shoulders and kissed my hair. I was conscious that I hadn't washed it for a couple of days.

"Good to see you," he said.

"You too," I told him, because it was. But I didn't look at him, I looked at our reflections in the window.

"You look good."

"You too."

"Do you need anything?"

"No." Yes. I need a home, a job, I need my brother back. "I'm doing okay."

"Are you sure Alix? You look a little..."

"A little what?"

"Well, a little starved. A little emaciated."

He said emaciated, but I heard the little boy inside say "emancipated" and I laughed.

"What?"

"I was just thinking... Remember when we were kids? And you used to think it was emancipated?"

He smiled a little.

"Yeah. All the emancipated children in Africa. I couldn't understand what all the fuss was about."

The train lurched and we lurched with it. Some of his perfectly styled ash blond hair fell in front of his eyes. I wished I could get my hair to look that good. He pushed it back with his free hand, and I looked closer at the part of his face that had been hidden.

"Asher," I said. "You have lines!"

He pushed the hair back down.

"No I don't."

"Yes you do. There's crow's feet just like Aunt Jessum used to get."

"Crow's feet are okay," he told me. "Crow's feet are from laughing."

But I knew his weren't. Asher was taken from the womb only minutes before I was, but he was worlds and worlds older.

"You're getting old." I poked him; not hard, not menacingly, but he winced anyway.

The train door flew open and a cold burst of air blew in. I shivered and pulled my hat out of my pocket. Asher looked at it critically.

"You're still wearing the same hat."

"So?"

"When was the last time you bought something new for yourself?"

"I like this old hat."

"When was the last time you bought something new?"

"Last week," I lied. The door shut and we moved on, sliding over tracks rubbed smooth with a thousand journeys, a million conversations. The train burst out of the ground, and for a few minutes we were surrounded by the city. I looked out on the lights and saw our world, Asher's and mine. I saw the buildings reflected in the river, and in the reflection I saw a nightmare world, where up was down and everything was dark and shaky. I saw the world outside the train, the world we were about to enter.

"Look," Asher pointed to a tall sparkling building. "That's where I work."

I heard: "That's where they keep me."

"You're not going back, are you?" I hadn't meant to say it. Not yet anyway. I had meant to save it for later in the trip, after we reminisced about our shared childhood and dozed off to the rocking of the train. I had meant to ruin the peace at the end of our trip, not the beginning of it.

"Alix." He stopped pointing and took his arm off my shoulders. "You don't understand."

"No," I said, meaning "Yes."

"I had to make money. I can't live like you."

"We're still wearing the same shoes."

"No Alie, you're wearing the same shoes. Mine are a new pair, just last year." I felt unexpected tears prick up in the well of my eye, but I knew how to keep them from falling.

"How can you do this?" I was shouting at Asher, but I felt like I was shouting at the whole city. "How can you be so—so resolute? How can you just accept everything?"

"I'm accepting everything? You're the one who goes North for so many years and lives in the cold, refusing to get a job or even buy new clothes!"

"You're the one who lets suits order him around all day, never standing up for yourself!"

"You don't even have a place to live!"

"You don't even have a life to live!"

The train was sucked back underground, sucking away any words Asher might have said. I might have seen a tear in his eye, but Asher doesn't cry. It would ruin his face. I don't cry because of living up North; there were times when it would be so cold that if you cried, tears would freeze to your face and you would have to scrape off the ice with your fingernails. Asher doesn't know physical discomfort. He has never slept in furs, he sleeps in a climate controlled gray walled apartment. A woman comes every other week to vacuum his gray rugs and dust his gray curtains. He has never eaten whale blubber, he eats sushi, and he eats it with chopsticks. He drinks vodka in elegant crystal glasses because it is what the suits have told him to do. He has never drank vodka because the burn of the liquid down your throat and into your tingling fingers may be the warmest thing you'll feel all day. The only discomfort Asher knows is the discomfort of the soul.

I felt him turn to stare at me, and as one we shifted our feet up onto the seat, sitting cross legged so we could watch each other. We sat knee to knee, my left against his right, the way we always sat.

"Your gloves don't have fingers." He touched one.

"Your coat doesn't have a lining." I felt it with my fingerless gloves. The inside of his coat was smooth. He wouldn't last a week up north.

He put his hand on top of our knees, and I put mine on top of his. We leaned our foreheads together. This is the way we sat in our fort, when we were just little kids.

"How old were you?" he asked. "How old were you when you realized all the possibilities closed to you? When you realized you were too old to have smoking a cigarette be illegal and exciting, that you could just go down to the store and buy one? When you realized you're a twenty year old virgin, and you'll never be able to have hot teenage sex? When you realized you couldn't be president because your parents weren't born in America?"

"That's wrong, Asher," I told him, "You can still be president."

"Oh?"

"Only you have to be American born."

"There's one, anyway." I felt the skin on his forehead wrinkle against mine. "But doesn't it depress you? That all these opportunities were there and now they're not? All those possibilities lost?"

"I read a lot up North." I said. "Sometimes it was too cold to do anything else, and the snow and the ice were so blinding that all you could do was stay in your furs and read. I read one book, the author talked about parallel universes. It said that there are an infinite number of universes, all overlapping each other, all seeming the same at first, but as they get farther and farther apart, they get more and more different. With every choice you make, the you in one of those other universes makes the choice a different way." I squeezed his hand. "So somewhere else, a seventeen year old you had sex with a really hot girl and smoked a cigarette afterwards."

101

He laughed at that. It was just a little laugh, but I felt a part of him come back. Like a piece of the Asher in one of those parallel universes, one who hadn't decided to conform and get a job, and apartment, and an unlined coat, had taken pity on my Asher and sent a little piece of himself through the overlapping universes to me.

"The way I see it," I said, "All the possibilities are being played out. None of them really ever closed to you."

When Asher and I were born, our knees were fused together; his right to my left. The bones were separate, but it took several operations until all the muscles and skin was sorted out evenly. My knee twinges sometimes, and I always think of Asher. I call it my "thinking knee." He calls it his "feeling knee." There is literally a part of me in him, and a part of him in me. I sometimes wonder if we weren't meant to be just one person. If maybe having two children like us instead of just one was what finally drove our mother away; if maybe our being so close had less to do with being all each other had, and more to do with being the same person. I pictured us in my head, little blond babies, a two headed monster sleeping on our mother's shabby couch. Growing up, I had always wanted to be Asher. But maybe I already was.

The moon rose, hovered and sank, and the train continued its endless circles into the night. Asher fell asleep with his feet in my lap, and I played with the buttons of his coat while he slept. I still wanted to be him, if only to get up and walk out of his life. I wondered if he felt the same about me. I wondered what would happen if we switched places for a day, a month, a year. Would either one of us survive? No one was checking up on us, making sure we were still alive in the first place. How long would it take before someone found the bones, matched up the skeletons, saw the identical knees? We had been riding this train since we were little kids, but we were still strangers here. This city would always be foreign to us.

"Wake up." I shook his foot. "We have to leave."

"It's not dawn yet. Is it?"

It wasn't yet, but I could feel it coming, in the way the metal around the seats was colder, the train emptier, the air crisper.

"Let's get on another train."

"Another train?"

"One that's leaving the city."

"I have to work on Monday."

"Asher."

"How did you know? How did you know I quit?"

I poked at him.

"My thinking knee told me."

"My feeling knee must have sent out signals."

"I can't stand watching you die."

He sat up sharply and slapped my face, hard. He twisted my hair around his hands, but instead of yanking it, he pulled me towards him, until suddenly we were embracing, and our knees were pressed together so tightly it was like we were back in the womb.

"I'm going." he said. "I already have a ticket."

I couldn't speak. I knew it was coming, but I hadn't known it would be this real.

"I love you" was all I could say.

The sun was rising, the ride was over. We stepped off the train, wobbling a bit at the sudden stillness of the platform.

"Where will you go?" I asked.

"Someplace warm. Someplace south."

I kissed him goodbye, and watched him walk away. He limped slightly, favoring his right leg.

Please, I implored the city. This time, let him go.

The Mall

1. THE STONE BOY IN THE FOUNTAIN

They meet by the fountain in the middle of the mall, where once bloomed a thick green canopy woven with birds, but now stands a glittery plastic model of a stone boy, water spewing out of the fish he holds in his hands.

The boys' hands are green, but it's not the green of pleasant mosses and coppery rust; it's the green of Hot Topic nail polish and wayward highlighters, of sale stickers and plastic house plants. He is fake, and he can't help it. He doesn't know any better.

The stones that make up the pool are fake. They are the hollowed out painted rubber of hide-a-key rocks. No one knows it, but there is a key inside each one. They can no longer remember what they go to. Maybe castles, maybe treasure chests, maybe just old suitcases and lawn mowers. They sleep inside their rubber rocks.

There is a girl who loves the plasticine boy. She comes to visit him whenever she can. She is the one responsible for the nail polish on his arms and fingernails. She is short, and it is as high as she can reach. She spent an entire afternoon wearing her mother's vintage platform boots and painting his fingernails day-glo orange. The next time she came back, someone had painted every other nail purple.

It is, in fact, Hot Topic nail polish. It's not that she really likes Hot Topic, but once she really needed a plaid skirt when she was shopping with her aunt, and it is this same aunt who now gives her a gift card every birthday, and the same aunt who has yet to notice that the plaid skirt is the only new thing her niece has bought in three years. She doesn't want to waste the gift cards, so she buys things for the stone

105

boy; nail polish and bangles, and once a tweedy brimmed hat that, as it turns out, she was too short to put on the statues' head. So she gave it to her brother, and, after the bangles went missing, decided to stick to nail polish and other more permanent attire. Once she bought a dozen tiny rhinestone earrings, took off the backs, and stuck them into the rocks under the water. This girl is the only one who has bothered to figure out that the rocks in the fountain are not actually made of rock.

The water, however, is real. Everyone has noticed this; because it has a weird smell. A smell the people in the mall can't quite place, because it does not smell like detergent or plastic or cologne. It smells like the earth. The real earth, the primal earth, the earth that the people remember from ancestral bonfires and tribal hunts. It smells like bloodlust and tree rot. It smells alive, but not for long.

2. THEM

When they come to the Mall, they have to sneak through the glass and under the metal bars. It's no secret; they come to steal babies. They hang out in babyGap and the toddler section of Sears, smelling of overripe strawberries and burning leaves. They can't touch the babies while you're there, holding the baby's hand, stroking their hair, feeding them cheerios from little plastic baggies. But the minute you step away—the very second your eyes glance to the side, or you stop to finger those ridiculously tiny cloth shoes and your little one walks on without you—that's the minute They wait for.

When you put that car seat on the floor for just a second while you pay the cashier, it's already too late. They have hands like spiders with golden fingertips, and They burn smokey holes in the upholstery when They get too excited. And it's hard not to be excited at the prospect of a new baby.

106

And it's not like the stories of old, where a sticky, sickly changeling is left in place of the healthy human baby. There's no doll or facsimile left behind. Only burn marks like cigarettes; finger sized holes around the buckle that might cause child services to wonder, after all, if you might have lost the baby without anyone's help.

But you'll know.

The loss doesn't feel real at first, but that clinging panic—that feels real. The cloying, fruity smell that you can't seem to get out of the car after you put the baby seat back in might not be real. But the finger burns are real; the singed threads of where the seat belt used to hold together are real.

And you cry at night, because you know someone took her. You hope she's alright; that her body isn't covered in burns like her car seat. You know you didn't lose her. And when you hold the little dress you were buying when she disappeared sometimes you can smell the smoke of leaves. Sweet as milk, but bitter too.

3. TOO HOT

It's only April and it's already too hot to be outside. The ground scorches and hums with an electric heat so intense I can feel it through my shoes. Only a few years ago I remember playing outside until June or July, we'd play soccer and stickball and four square in the streets and parking lots, but now the blacktop melts when you touch it, and if you stand on it too long you start to sink down down down into this enormous tar pit. Like how the dinosaurs died.

We live in a trailer outside of Burnsie. It's made mostly of tin, or aluminum, or some other kind of sheet metal. When it's about eleven o'clock, the sun is in just the right position to start heating up the roof and eastern walls. The light bounces around like off a magnifying glass

107

or a mirror, and once last August it caught the grass on fire and our front steps burned down. Now we have concrete cinder blocks stacked up for a staircase and we keep the grass cut real short and always have a fire extinguisher ready.

The walls are so thin and the inside so dark that everything heats up real fast with all that sun shining on it, and by twelve thirty or one it's too hot to be inside, hotter even than the air outside, and so humid that your hair curls and your eyeballs start to sweat and the soles of your feet get so slippery that you can't keep your flip flops on your feet no matter what you try. Then we have to run for the car, the old car with the front upholstery burned off from the sun and the back seat smelling like wet mold, and the air conditioner fried years ago so that you can never decide if it's better or worse to leave the windows open.

But it's all worth it when we get to the mall.

The mall is a sweet cool oasis where the wind that blows is cold and smells like plastic and cinnamon. We try to eat only the coldest foods when we visit there: lemonade and frozen snickers bars and the ice cream that comes in tiny colored beads. We like to sit by the fountain where the stone boy with the fish lives. We can put our feet in the water and wash the tar off our shoes until the security guard shoos us away.

Then we wander through the stores where unruffled black and white models smile coolly down from larger than life posters; their clothing billowing in the breeze by the lake which would in reality cover them with ash or burn them with ozone. At the very least their pretty bare feet should be blistered and puckered and dented with sand.

We have never seen the ocean, but in the mall advertisements we imagine it as it once was. Sometimes we like to try on swimsuits and stand in front of an air vent, just to watch the goosebumps prickle our skin. We lick the salt off pretzels and pretend it is the sea. We turn drinking fountains up too high and try to catch the spray on the lenses of our borrowed sunglasses.

It is not the sea and it never will be, but when we lay in the massage chairs and drink our strawberry smoothies, we can pretend.

Because what is the mall, if not a land of pretend? Even ordinary people, non-aluminum trailer people, come here to pretend. That they have money, that they have somewhere to wear those fancy clothes. That they can fit into that size they used to wear.

We like to think we are better than them. That we appreciate the mall more. That it is our Mecca, our Valhalla, our Heaven. When we die, be it of old age, disease or heat stroke, we would like to go to a place like the Mall. Our souls would like to laze by the fountain and watch the people go by. We think we could do it. Spend an eternity in this plastic paradise.

4. A PROBLEM, MR. GREASE

"Mr. Grease," she said, "I'm glad you could come." Her tone is clipped, blank, professional. She wears a gray suit dress and black rimmed glasses. Her dark hair is pulled up into a tight, no nonsense bun. I don't know if I like her.

"No problem," I say. "It's kind of my job." Her eyes flick to the left. I think my casual tone makes her uncomfortable.

"Ma'am." I add. Her eyes flick again.

"Miss." I look away so I can't see if she continues to twitch.

"What can I do you for?"

She sighs and apparently gives up.

"There is a problem, Mr. Grease," she is dramatic, "With the fountain."

"The one with the boy peeing?"

109

She sighs again. She is like a caricature of an exasperated schoolteacher. Does she take off her glasses and let down her hair and turn into a sex goddess?

I wonder what kind of underwear she's wearing. I can't help it. Is it a red surprisingly sexy kind? Is it gray and structured like her suit? Does it button up the front? I giggle at this. She's probably twitching her eyes at me.

"The *Youth Holding Fish* is not—*urinating*—Mr. Grease. The fish in his arms is spewing forth water, most likely in reference to some sort of Oceanic-based horn of plenty—"

"Yeah, yeah," I interrupt. I know all this. Everybody knows this. But from a certain angle he does look like he's peeing.

"The problem, Mr. Grease—actually there are several problems— the major problem is the smell."

"The smell?" I ask. I feel like a detective from a pulp novel. I imagine I've got a little notebook and maybe a pipe. Some shiny shoes.

"The water coming out of the fish smells very strange."

"Something's fishy," I say. She is not amused. My shoes are actually worn out, shit brown flip flops, and my feet are freezing in the air conditioning.

"And the other thing—someone keeps painting the statue with some sort of permanent ink that we can't wash off. We were hoping you may have some sort of super powerful cleaning solution you might be able to use." It is funny to hear this woman use the word "super." It makes her sound like a perky teenage girl.

"I'll see what I can do." I tell her. What I want to tell her is that it's not a real statue. It's made of plastic. Those flecks aren't mica, they're synthetic glitter. And I've never even liked the real *Youth Holding Fish* statue. The boy's inhuman face and strangely large hands creep me out a little. I wouldn't mind the little fucker getting a paint job. Hell, I'd help out.

"We really appreciate it." How she can walk so fast in heels I can't imagine. My left flip flop thong is stretched out and threatening to detach from the bottom. I can barely keep up.

"People expect to see *Youth Holding Fish* when they visit the Burnsie Area Mall. They expect to see him unmarred by pranksters. They do not expect to smell him."

As we start to get closer to the statue, I can see what she means. The smell isn't unpleasant, exactly. It's just strange. Alien in this enclosed space. It reminds me of the way my grandparent's house smelled; back when I was very small. They had a window box where they grew string beans. The water smells like the bean plants smelled when Gram and Grandpa waited too long to pick them; sweet and earthy and a little uncomfortable. It was a smell that burned all the way to the back of the tongue and didn't want to leave in the usual way. I decide a cherry smoothie is probably in order before I start this job.

"As you can see, Mr. Grease, it's rather overpowering."

I nod in agreement and forget to be a smart ass. She smiles a little. Her eyes behave like a normal person's for a moment.

"I'll see what I can do," I say again, and this time I really mean it. The smell is making me feel weird. Not nauseous exactly, but uncomfortable in my brain.

"Maybe it's in the pipes." I say in my best detective voice. I put down my toolkit and stretch my arms up over my head so I can loosen that kink in my shoulder, but also so she can how tight my muscles have gotten since I took this job. "Maybe something crawled in there and died."

The eyes flick again. Shoot, I've ruined the moment. Oh well. She probably just has normal, boring underwear on under there anyway.

5. KOI

It's a little too small. He kicks and kicks his tail, and scooches forward a half centimeter at a time. Up ahead, he can see a bend in the pipe, getting infinitesimally closer. He kicks again, but he's getting tired, weaker. His fat little body has blocked up the pipe too well, and the water around him is trickling by. His face is drying out. His gills pump in the air; needing oxygen, needing water. He kicks his tail harder and harder and shoves his weight forward, just a little. He tries to blink but his eyes are too dry. Everything starts to spin and fade away, he feels like he is floating above himself.

Hurry, the others think at him. For a moment he doesn't want to answer; want to stay stuck forever and float off to whatever is next. But then he remembers why he has come here. He remembers the great pleasure he will have when he holds one in his arms, when his mission is complete.

Stuck. He manages. *Push.*

Fat? says someone.

Fat. he says back. *Fat fat fatfatfat.* Later, his fat will be good. He has been proud of his body; the sleek muscle and the rippling scales. He could breech himself using only his tail. He was the strongest, so he went first.

Push, they say behind him. *Push push pushpushpush.* But it may already be too late. His vision is turning black; dark storm clouds coming from all directions. He feels hot. He feels cold. Someone bites him on the tail and he comes back.

Kick, he hears, and he can feel them kicking behind him, a great wave of glittery blacks and whites and golds, all those little bodies

112

pulsing together as one, and he starts to slide a little and the water that slips out around him is cold and wet. And they come to the bend in the pipe, and he shouts *Bend!* with his renewed energy from the mass behind him, and the mass behind him shouts *Bend bend bendbendbend!* back at him. They push and push and he feels a great tear in his right fin. The pain is searing, blinding, and his vision flickers even worse than before. He can feel the scales scraping off, tearing and ripping along his side and over his back and he wants to shout at them to *stop pushing!* but he knows the only way this will ever stop for good is to let them push him out into the water.

And they do.

When he is free of the pipe, at first he doesn't even know it. He lays stunned at the bottom of the pool, barely breathing. The water seeps over him, and slowly begins to moisten again. He can hear the *plop plop* of the other fish falling from the pipe, can hear them squeal with glee and splash and wiggle. Someone comes up beside him and nudges gently against his wounded size. The pain still bubbles there but the water has cooled it.

Is it bad? she asks.

He can barely answer. He just wants to float until it all feels better.

6. THE BABY IN THE STROLLER

The baby in the stroller is the only one who sees the fish plop out of the pipe into the fountain. He giggles and claps his hands and kicks his little baby feet. His mother is talking to a friend and doesn't see what he sees. She rocks his stroller back and forth, tipping it up on its back wheels and then down to the floor again. The motion is like the motion of the waves. He swims like the fish in the fountain; up and down and up and down. The fish look at him. They swim towards the edge of the

113

fountain, lining up like soldiers. Then, as the baby watches, they start to change.

There's a little ripple around each fish, which blend together on the surface of the water and soon it is dappled as if by raindrops. The underside of the fountain gleams reflectively and there's a flash like a camera, and little men start climbing out of the fountain. The water steams off of them, and they shake their hair dry.

Their limbs are long and thin like sticks, and they are the color of sticks too. They scamper like cockroaches over the floor towards the baby, and he stops giggling as they get closer, and breathes in his breath to scream and then they are upon him, hands burning like little knives, sawing through the restraints, carrying him off around the side of the fountain.

His mother feels the weight difference when she tips the stroller back again, but by then, of course, it is too late.

7. SHE SCREAMS

She screams, of course, and people look up, in unison, but it is still late. Everyone smells strawberry and smoke, but they never find the baby.

8. THEN

Never before had they attempted such a daring move in such a public place. The plan with the fountain was treacherous but ultimately more successful than they could ever have dreamed. They will try again soon. They will slip through water fountains and soda machines and air conditioning vents. But tonight they have to get their precious bounty back home. Their bounty screams and squalls as they take turns holding him, but he cries a little softer at each burn.

In the morning the strange earthy smell from the water in the fountain is gone. Instead there is a fruity, plasticy smell which is mostly camouflaged by the smoothie stand across the food court and the perfumery upstairs. When the plumber kicks the children out of the fountain to get a closer look at pipes, he notices an orange and yellow fish flopping in underneath the spray. It swims in circles, bumping into the sides. One of its fins is missing.

The plumber buys a smoothie and drinks it while he makes a call on his cell phone. He sits on the fake rocks and slurps up the icy red syrup through a clear straw. When he is finished, he rinses out the cup and scoops up the orange and black fish. He has a nephew he thinks will like it.

And as the day turns into evening and the food court begins to empty, one small girl in a plaid skirt is left, painting the fountain boy's fingernails gold and smearing strawberry lotion onto his dry, dry skin.

The Dead Do Not Come Back at Night

I.

Uncle says the dead do not come back at night.

Uncle is wrong.

Uncle says the voices that I hear each night

are not real.

They are just my mind

Playing tricks

or my dreams

coming early.

They are not the dead.

Not at all.

Definitely not.

But in the basement, Uncle

has a shrine,

to Aunt, who I never met,

who died

with Mother

and Father

in the boating accident when I was just a baby.

Aunt

has long blond hair that's all in one braid.

She has lots of straight teeth

and she looks tall, although it's hard to tell in just a photograph.

Uncle put potpourri in a little glass jar next to the photo.

In front of them are:

a strand of yellowy pearls,
a metal statue of a pony,
a music box that plays Yankee Doodle Dandy,
and five candies that look like peppermints
but are actually cinnamon.
(there used to be six)

Uncle
doesn't know that I used to visit Aunt
almost every single night.
He thinks I stopped when he told me too,
after I ate that cinnamon candy
and he yelled at me
and almost cried.
But she is nice to talk to
when Uncle isn't there,
and besides,
there are no shrines for my
Mother and Father,
so who else will listen to me?

But I have seen her.
Her hair is very pale
and she likes to sing.

II.

My Mother,

so they say,

was not as pretty as my Aunt.

Her teeth were not as straight,

and her hair was not as blond.

She was the Ugly Twin,

my Grandma used to say

even though

they were not twins at all.

They used to sing in a choir,

and Grandma would make them do duets

even though they hated it;

standing

back to back in front

of all those people and dressed exactly alike.

Warbling like little birds in a cage

everyone in the choir behind them

jealous but scornful.

Aunt sang the national anthem at a ball game once.

Mother was sick and stayed home.

They didn't even bring her funnel cake.

III.

Uncle

does not like to talk about my Father.

They did not get along.

My Father was too quiet

and he made Uncle nervous.

They would sit together

in Uncle's two puffy chairs

and not say anything

for hours.

IV.

I do not tell anyone that Aunt is dead.

If anyone asks

I tell them that I live with both Uncle and Aunt.

They do not ask if Aunt lives

so I do not have to tell them.

She comes to me at night

and she sings.

Sometimes it is lullabies

but mostly

it is the National Anthem.

Her voice is whispery and feathery,

and I do not see why she and Mother sang so many duets

but maybe it was better when she was alive.

But right now

she sounds like me when I have a cold.

Uncle heard her once, although he will not admit it.

He heard her and he banged on my wall

and told me

to Stop All That Racket and

Go To Sleep God Damn It.

When I told him it was Aunt

he wouldn't speak to me for days,

only to say

Pass The Milk

and

Time For School.

But I bet he recognized her.
I bet he did.
I bet he misses her
even more than I miss my Mother
and Father
because he knew Aunt for a lot longer
than I knew either of them.
But that is no excuse for ignoring someone.

In school we make drawings of our families.
Mom, Dad, Dog, Cat, House.
I draw Uncle and Aunt,
a house and a basement,
no pets because Uncle is allergic and says I am too
Even though I have not sneezed even once
ever
in my whole life and maybe longer.

The teachers say
Oh
and
Ah
and
Is That Your Mommy and Daddy?
and I have to start all over again.

V.

The counselor asks me what my favorite subject is

and I tell her Recess,

and she tells me that is not really a subject and try again.

So I think really hard

and finally I say

Art?

And she nods and smiles and gives me some paper to draw on.

But I really just like Art because I like it when we do clay.

I like to smash it down really flat

and then put the flat piece over my face and try to blow a bubble.

That must be what it is like for Aunt

dead down at the bottom of that lake

water pressing all around her face.

I ask for clay, but the counselor says

Next Time, Let's Draw,

so I draw Aunt

down there

having a tea party with Mother and Father.

They are all blue.

Counselor says

Who Are They?

and I tell her how

Aunt is taking a visit to Mother and Father in the lake,

but she will be home by bedtime

to sing to me.

Counselor says

Oh.

None of the other drawings on her walls are like mine.

They are all Mom Dad Brother Cat

and Mom Dad Sister Dog Doghouse

like the other kids in my class.

I tell her she can keep mine

to add to her collections.

And she says

Thanks

and

Back To Class Now

and

See You Again Next Week.

So I go back to class

and I skip on my right foot

but my left foot won't do it.

VI.

Next week, Counselor has brought clay

but it's not the gray stuff that smells like dirt that we use in class,

it's little kid stuff that smells like plastic.

There is bright green and bright pink

and bright blue

and I choose blue

and I pound it out flat on Counselor's desk

while she asks me questions she already know the answers too,

like

How Old Were You When They Died

and

Do You Have Bad Dreams

and

Are The Other Kids Nice To You.

When the clay is all flat

I show her my bubble trick.

I put the clay over my face

and for a second the world is cool and dark

but when I take a breath to try to blow out a bubble

I accidentally get some clay in my mouth

and the taste is chemically and all wrong

not like the mud at the bottom of the lake.

It makes me gag

and I know I shouldn't

but I spit and spit

and there is blue all over the bottom of her trashcan.

That's Okay

she tells me

It's Part Of The Process.

and

I Think We're Having A Real Breakthrough Here.

VII.

That night, I try to get my Aunt to sing

My Bonny Lies Over The Ocean

but she won't say anything.

I don't even see her.

I think she is visiting Mother and Father

or maybe Uncle is down at her shrine

and she wants to have some alone time with him.

So I have to sing it myself.

I start off really quiet,

just laying there and humming.

thinking maybe I can make myself fall asleep.

Then I get excited because I remember

you can replace the word Bonny with Body

and then the song is funny

instead of sad.

So then I am singing louder and louder

and jumping on the bed

singing in my best loud choir opera singer voice

that my Body Lies Over The Ocean

My Body Lies Over The Sea

and right when I am at the best part,

shouting

Bring BACK Bring BACK

Uncle comes in

my door flies open

he turns on the light and it's too bright

CUT THAT OUT

he yells,

and his yells are louder than my BACKs.

He slams the door and I am so startled

I stop jumping

and lay down

my heart pounding

harder than 100 dead people dying.

But I can't hold back a little giggle.

And he hears it

and he says

Katie

in his warning voice, and thumps on the wall

just once

to remind me

And I wish he would come jump with me

Just once

But he can't.

VII.

Counselor says

Wait

Let's Feed The Fish

Before I Send You Back to Class

and she shows me

how to grab just a pinch of brown and yellow fish flakes

that smell like salt and animal poo

and sprinkle it into the tank.

The fish come up

with their mouths like funnels

and O it into themselves.

They don't even chew.

VIII.

Did the fish eat Mother and Father and Aunt

after they died?

Were there lake fish

and snails

and bugs

that snacked on them the same way

I eat my yogurt and my Triscuits

every day at 10:30?

Did it hurt them?

Can they feel it still?

IX.

I ask Uncle

about the fish

but he doesn't answer.

He grunts a little

and gets up from the table

before his plate is cleared.

I tried that once

and he made me sit a whole hour

maybe two

all alone at the table

until I ate it all.

It wasn't even that I don't like carrots.

I was just full.

After dinner

I sneak down to the shrine

while Uncle is watching the news.

I pick up some of the potpourri between my fingers

just like Counselor showed me

and I squish it up really small

and sprinkle it on the photo of Aunt.

Afterwards,

my fingertips smell like roses.

X.

Counselor has the idea

that Uncle should take me to the graveyard.

I say that I don't want to go.

I tell them both.

But no one listens.

Actually, Counselor told Uncle

that he and Aunt

should both take me.

I was listening.

Uncle told Counselor

that Aunt was Dead

and Counselor was all quiet

for a very long time.

I thought maybe Aunt

had zipped down the phone lines to find her

but it turns out that Counselor was just surprised.

She had thought Aunt was alive.

When I tried to explain it to her later,

how Aunt lived with us but was not alive,

she ignored me

and told me to draw a new picture.

So I drew gravestones at night

in a tornado.

Everything was black.

It was very scary.

XI.

The night before we go to the graveyard

I dream about seaweed

wrapping around me

while Mother and Aunt sing the Star Spangled Banner.

It is much scarier than my drawing

(which I also gave Counselor to hang up on her wall)

But in my dream

Uncle is there

and he tells them to

Hush

just like he tells me all the time.

And that makes it better somehow.

And when I wake up

I am not covered in seaweed

but the rain is coming in through my window screen

and my blanket is wet.

XII.

I ask Uncle if I can take some paper and some crayons

and do a grave rubbing.

He says Okay

even though I can see in his eyes

that he does not know what a grave rubbing is.

It's cold outside so I wear my black jacket,

which is good for me because it has big pockets

where I can store the crayons.

We park in a dirt lot

with a metal fence around it.

Uncle takes my hand

which he never does

and we walk a really long way

through lots of headstones

and one big statue of a sad looking lady

until we reach three gray graves that all match.

They say their names.

The names of

Aunt

Mother

Father.

Uncle picks up some stones and puts them on top of the graves.

He puts the most on Aunt's.

I want to know if their bodies are in there.

Yes

says Uncle.

His voice sounds funny,

like it's stretched really tight.

So Mother and Father are not down at the bottom of the lake.

No

says Uncle

They Are Buried Here

Like Normal People Who Die.

I can't even believe it.

I get really excited.

The fish are not eating them

Their bones are not washing around down there

in the mud and the sand.

They are here

with me

where I can come and visit them

and even stand on top of them if I want to.

I get out my crayons

and my paper

and show Uncle how to do a grave rubbing.

It is really windy

so he has to help me hold the paper while I do it.

Mother's name

appears like a ghost itself

slowly darkening in purple

which is the color of rich velvet curtains

and sour sweet grapes

and dark bruises.

Father
is a dark green
like the forest
and damp moss
and growing things everywhere.
His name
is longer
and I think I am going to run out of room
but at the last second
I don't.

And last I do Aunt
in quiet brown
like photo of her in the frame in the shrine
and what the potpourri has turned too
and what my Uncle's eyes look like
when they are too sad.

I give that one to Uncle
and he smiles a little
and frowns a little
and turns his back to me
so I can't see him wipe off his eyes.
When he isn't looking
I steal one of the stone off the grave.
It is smooth and warm
brown like Aunt

and I can feel it pulling my coat down to the right

when I put it in my pocket.

I can feel her around me

in the air

she wants it

but she can't touch it

she can't have it

not yet.

I'll give it to her tonight

at the shrine.

Maybe she can go to it

curl up inside it like an egg

and someday hatch out again.

Or maybe when he dies

Uncle can join her

and I can carry them around in my pocket forever.

XIII.

Afterwards

I ask Uncle if we can have a picnic

at the grave.

I saw it once in a movie

and it looked like the right thing to do.

Uncle says he doesn't have any food

but then he remembers a package of chips

under the driver's seat.

we go get them

together

and when I take his hand

he doesn't take it back again.

And I wonder why Aunt came back

but not my parents.

I want to ask Uncle

but I think I know the answer anyway.

We walk back to the graves

and we open the bag of chips.

It is just a mini one

and it's a little smashed

but the insides are good and salty.

The grease stays heavy on the back of my tongue.

I kiss the graves

and my mouth leaves a shiny print each time

getting fainter

as I go down the line.

Then I lie in the grass in their shade.

"Can we come back again?"
I ask Uncle.
He thinks for a minute.
He watches me
and he watches Aunt
and he looks up in the sky
where the sun is still shining.
And he doesn't look so mad anymore.
And he says
"Okay."

Shimmering

Part I

Cara and I are at the lake

My parents have taken us for the day

The summer is so hot

The only relief we have is the waters murky coolness

By August it will be like a bath

We sit on the dock

We laugh,

We play,

There is no one else here in this secluded spot

No one else has discovered our paradise

Don't tell Brody I whisper to Cara

If her brother knew

He would destroy our little Eden

Bring his little boy friends

With their loud screams and splashes

Ruin our secluded peace

It gets ruined anyway

Nat

An old friend

From years ago

I've almost forgotten

He comes with others

Carl
Joseph
Bret

Cara, in her two-piece
Admires them
But we keep our distance
Shy of people we used to know

I am remembering an old legend
And I tell it to the group
Trying to connect the bridge
Of our past selves to our present

When you swim out past the striped rock, I say
You disappear
Something from the deep grabs you
Cara looks at me
And laughs
To many Jaws movies she tells me
Nat told it to me I say, remembering in surprise
A long time ago
Nat laughs, remembering
And it is just like old times
Well says Cara
Let's see who gets snatched today

We sit on the dock
Eating watermelon

Watching the swimmers

Carl

Who is as old as my dad

Swims out to the legendary rock

He climbs on top

And stands triumphant

He rests

Then continues on

Past the striped rock

Cara nudges me

And we watch

Waiting to prove the old legend wrong

All we can see is Carl's head

As he swims

Then suddenly—

A smaller head

A man's head

A head that is shimmering

Appears behind Carl

Then they are both gone

Cara and I look at each other

The watermelon tastes sour

It drops from my hand into the lake with a soft splash

I half expect

Something smaller and shimmering

To some and snatch it

Did you see that? Cara whispers urgently

Did you see that?

I nod

Slowly

Unbelievingly

Should we say anything?

I shake my head

Who would we tell?

I ask

What would we say?

No one says anything about Carl

No one goes to look for him

Or even ask where he has gone

We talk and laugh as before

But the silences grow

More frequent

And longer

And it isn't the same as it used to be

Maybe it never was

Then someone starts a game

A silly game, really

Stand straight

Ramrod straight

And fall backwards into the water

Without flinching

Whoever does it the most times wins

Many times we go around the circle

And no one starts

We are acting like kids

And I feel a little embarrassed

But it is my turn again

So I start to fall

I look at Nat

Across the circle from me

And just for a moment

He changes

Shimmers

Like the man in the lake

Past the striped rock

Following Carl

I recoil

Like a reflex

Like getting your knee tapped at the doctor's office

And a spray of water goes up around me

You're out Zoe says Nat

But I don't care

Did you see how he shimmered, Cara?

Part II

Cara and I are sick

I feel like sleeping

All week long

Monday, Tuesday, Wednesday

Thursday

and Friday

But I know I can't

Cara's staying with us

While her parents bring Brody to summer school

And get him settled

We were supposed to have a whole weekend to ourselves

To games and sun and fun

But now it is all ruined

Mom set up the cot

In my room

On the other side of the dresser

Cara sleeps there still

Although the late morning sun filters through the curtains

I get up to use the bathroom

When I return

Cara has made a cocoon of the covers

Curled up

Facing the window

Her back to me

I reach for my water glass

It is not where I left it

I search the floor

Thinking I may have spilled it in my sleep

And there it is

But still upright

An inch of water coats the bottom

Has someone moved it then?

Beside it is another glass

Clear blue

There is water in it too

And in the bottom, a coating of shimmering powder

Like instant cocoa sediment

I shudder

I want nothing to do with anything shimmering

I pick up both cups and bring them to the bathroom

You're not going to dump those out? I hear a voice behind me

My father

Who is obsessive about conservation

No sir

I take a mouthful from the blue cup

Careful not to swallow

Who would put shimmering powder in a cup of water?

I turn around

My father is watching me

My father

I spit my mouthful in the sink

Not caring if he sees

The water shimmer as it goes down the drain

I fight the urge to swallow

My father

Part III

We are going to the zoo

They have done some work and it has reopened

With new exhibits

And my mother loves animals

We see the local ones first

Bear

Moose

Deer

They were here before

So we move on

There is a wooden suspension bridge over a gorge

It looks like something out of Indiana Jones

It looks like it will crumble when we cross it

We cross anyway

And it is surprisingly sturdy

Must be a trick, I think

Marketing

This way to small aquatic animals, the sign reads

Starfish

Urchins

Crabs

I watch with interest as a man marks numbers in a notebook

He looks official

I would like to stay longer, but we leave

My mother does not like small aquatic animals

Especially sea cucumbers

I think marine biologists are creepy, she says to me

As we cross another bridge

My father laughs

And asks us if we want to rent a glass bottomed boat

And go on the lake with him

The lake

I shudder

I am afraid of the lake now

Afraid the shimmering man will come again

Afraid he will take me with him this time

No I say

My mother agrees

We have not gotten to the best part of the zoo yet—

The exotic animals

My father shrugs and walks off by himself

He will be all alone

In his glass bottomed boat

And suddenly

I am suspicious

This is what he wanted all along

To be by himself

Out on the lake

So he can visit his shimmering friends

It was him that put the powder in your drink

He wants to make you like him

And Nat

And the man in the lake

You're next

Zoe,

You're next

We see all the exotics

My mother and I

Rhinos

Giraffes

A koala

Even the lion comes out of his den

Then my mother spots a sign

That wasn't there before

Giant elephants, she reads

This way

It must be the new exhibit

We can't resist

It's very strange

There are four enormous elephants in a pen

Slow moving giants

Their stomachs are above my head

I could walk under one

And it wouldn't even notice me

On a ledge behind the elephants

There is a fence
With more strange animals behind it
White
With black rings
Like tiger stripes, really
They look like ferocious dogs
With their curled up tails

Tigerdogs

The closest one
Who has been watching me all along
Lunges
And suddenly I know what will happen
He will land on top of me
And that will be the end
I draw my breath in fear
Of the inevitable
Barkgrowling ferociously he leaps
And is stopped short by a rope
He was tied all along

Let's go, I say to my mother

Part IV

I am afraid to eat or drink anything he gives me

I am afraid

It will have that strange powder in it

Strange powder that will make me shimmer

Like them

Part V

We are going out to dinner
A rare occasion
In this family anyway
Zoe let's go, my mother says
We are all waiting

I turn and ask
All?
Who is all?
Your father, she says
And some of his friends
Carl
You remember Carl?
He was at the lake that day
With Nat
Remember?

How could I forget?
Everything seems to blur a little
I think it's reality
Shifting from the one I know
To something new and terrifying

Hurry and get your socks dear, my mother says
So I hurry
I try
But my feet feel like lead
And my brain has turned to mud

I go up the stairs and into my room

I open the drawer in the dark

I have not turned a single light on

I do not need to

I know this house so well I could walk

Blindfolded

Through the rooms and not trip on anything

I grab my blue socks and turn to go

I pass the bathroom

My parent's room

The closet at the end of the hall

I am about to go down the stairs

When someone jumps out from the doorway

And grabs me

It is my father

It is Nat

It is Carl

Everything's blurring more

The dark

Which did not bother me before

Now prevents me from seeing

More than a pale outline of this man

Who has my forearms pinned in his grasp

The light from the kitchen downstairs

Is barely bright enough
To let me see him

Or maybe he is shimmering
Causing his own light

I yell as soon as he touches me
But no one comes
Who would?

No one is here

No one but the shimmering man

Atlantic City

When he arrived in Atlantic City, the first thing he did was order a gin and tonic. He had plans to sit at the window in his hotel room, the one that overlooked the beach, and let the waves and the sound of children's laughter soothe him. He called downstairs and was told that no alcoholic beverages would be served outside the bar until after five pm. He wanted to tell the annoyingly cheerful woman on the other end of the phone that this was Atlantic City. He wanted to tell her that the more alcohol he had in him, the more likely he would be to gamble away his money in the hotel lobby. He wanted to tell her she reminded him of his wife.

He didn't say any of these things. He sighed and pressed the fingers of his free hand to the bridge of his nose, trying to squeeze away the headache that seemed to have taken up permanent residence there. He closed his eyes and breathed in deeply, asked where the nearest liquor store was, and she gave him directions in that pert, chirpy voice with the accent that had to be fake, didn't it? No one talked like that. Not really. Not even in Atlantic City.

It was an effort of sheer willpower to put the phone back in the cradle, stand up off the bed. He was glad he hadn't taken off his shoes yet, the idea of bending down to reach them made his head swim. He cell phone beeped at him. It was running out of batteries, and he didn't have the charger. He turned it off and put it on the bureau, avoiding looking in the mirror.

Outside his room, the lights seemed too bright. In the lobby it was worse; sun shining, machines beeping and whirring, flashing images of coins and gems and dollar bills. His head began to pulse along with the neon sign with the picture of the bearded prospector and the cabaret

155

dancer. He made his way through a sea of old ladies, each one clutching a bag full of coins. Most of them had thin gray hair tinged with blue, but one had a shocking pink crew cut.

Outside was better. He could smell the ocean, though the row of hotels and shopping plazas blocked the sea from his view. The air was surprisingly crisp, colder than he'd expected. He had parked in the hotel's basement and gone to the lobby through an elevator, avoiding the outdoors altogether. He had let the sight of sunshine fool him into thinking it was warmer, or maybe it was just muscle memory from the other time he and Alex had been here; on a mid-July summer getaway steamy with tourists and seagulls.

At any rate, it was cold now and he didn't have a jacket. There was a bus parked outside the hotel, engine humming, the overweight driver sitting cozy inside with a book and a coffee. *Riverside Retirement Home—Where the Sun Always Shines!* was painted on the side. He imagined a daytime outing with the cluster of blue hairs inside; coins jangling, false teeth rattling, one pink crew cut leading them in songs from their childhood.

He put his hands in his pockets and slouched as the wind whipped around the corner of a building. It smelled like salt water, but also of metal. He felt his stomach turn. Was he smelling himself? He saw a souvenir shop next to liquor store and bought a tacky salmon colored t-shirt, which, under ordinary circumstances, he wouldn't be caught dead in. Then he went next door and bought the biggest, most expensive bottle of gin he could find, three limes, a pocket knife, and two bottles of tonic water.

When he went outside again the wind was at his back, and the smell was worse. He walked faster, as if could outrun it.

Inside the hotel, he had to go back down a few floors to the vending machines, where he filled his ice bucket too far and it overflowed, sending perfectly matched frozen mosaics tumbling along the carpet. He knelt down to pick them up and then realized there was nowhere to put them, so he left them in a rough pile, feeling vaguely guilty.

Back in the room, he unwrapped a plastic cup from the bathroom and put in two cubes of ice, a large wedge of lime, and equal parts of gin and tonic water. He took a sip and in the bright acidity he tasted Alex so hard that he almost spit out the drink. When the coughing had subsided he tried again. The second sip was easier, and the third easier than that. By the fourth he could actually swallow without hesitating, and by the fifth it tasted like a regular gin and tonic. By the sixth the drink was gone, and by the seventh the ice was between his teeth, crunching squeakily and making a nerve twinge in his sensitive back left molar.

He fixed another and sat down at the desk, pulling the chair out so he could swivel it towards the window. The view was the same as he remembered; pier to one side, endless boardwalk and beach on the other. They were building a shopping center on the pier, and this made him feel sad. He wondered if the ferris wheel at the end still worked, and this thought shot him through with such melancholy that he was paralyzed for a moment, couldn't blink even.

Of course there were no children on the beach, no sound of young laughter. It was March, and it was still too cold for all but a few beach goers, probably college students determined to be on a beach—any beach—during spring break. He had been a fool to come here. What was he doing? What was the point of the limes and the drinks and the tacky t-shirt still balled up in the bottom of the bag? He should be calling the police and his family and his lawyer. This was ridiculous.

But as he moved to pick up the phone he was frozen again. He

157

smelled that metallic perfume he'd noticed outside. Numb, he turned to look into the mirror, but it was another long breath before he could open his eyes. After only a second, he turned away, shaking. He had dropped the drink onto the carpet and only registered this fact as his foot stepped on the plastic cup, crunching it down and shooting a piece of ice under the bed. He went to the bathroom and turned on the water, stepping into the shower before it even had time to turn hot. Once it was scalding he scrubbed away at his skin, melting an entire bar of soap and emptying the miniature shampoo bottle.

It was a nice enough hotel to supply its guest with a bathrobe, even if it didn't serve alcohol before five. He put it on and sat on the closed toilet seat, thankful he'd run the hot water long enough that the mirror was fogged over. His face was only a white smear in front of him. He turned the water back on and opened the door, hoping it would be enough to obscure all the mirrors.

After a few minutes he retrieved his fallen plastic cup from its resting place on the rug, but found his foot had cracked the plastic beyond use. He went back to the bathroom to get another and found that with the door open, the condensation on the glass had begun to evaporate. With eight quick steps he was out, back at the desk by the window, back firmly turned to the room. He poured more gin, and noticed his hands were red and shaking.

It was time. (Was it time?) He reached for the phone, but found he hadn't moved at all. He shot his drink all in one go, and realized as he swallowed he had forgotten the tonic, the lime. Alex burned all the way down his throat, into his belly, shooting stars out from his chest. The people on the beach would have been blinded, but they had all gone home.

He picked up his shirt, his pants, unfolded them across the bed so that they lay, human shaped, on the left side. Alex's side. The pants were torn at the knee, just a tiny little tear, a rough patch, really. If they had been jeans no one would have been able to tell. He touched the hole, brushed at, tried to close it with nothing more than willpower. Then he smoothed the shirt, the once tan button up, now splattered red with blood. He smoothed it over and over again, but the stains were mostly dry and set, only brief smudges clung to his fingertips.

The smell was all around him now. The hot smell of metal and oil and blood. It rose from the shirt like a vapor and he fled to the bathroom.

With one hand, one shaking, red tipped, bruised and battered hand, he wiped away the rest of the shower steam from the mirror.

And there he was.

On closer inspection, he didn't look much different. Paler, maybe. Darker under the eyes. And of course there were the bruises and scrapes; a purple line running from his left shoulder towards his hip where the seatbelt had cut into him, a split lip where his chin had hit the steering wheel, the swelling from what might turn out to be a cracked rib. But fundamentally, he was still whole, still unchanged, whereas Alex was gone, left behind, an entirely empty person.

He walked back to the bed and retrieved the tacky pink shirt, slipped it on with his boxers. Then he picked up the phone, dialed those three digits, so firmly ingrained in his memory he was able to dial them without even looking at the phone, eyes locked instead on his own reflection.

"There's been an accident," he said when someone picked up.

He tried to touch his face through the glass but there was no one there.

The Worst Part

After it was all over, he had to go back and tell their parents. This was the worst part. To see their excitement as they saw his beat up silver station wagon and came out to meet it, ready to help unload the weekend's bags and supplies. Then their confusion as they saw the lone teenager in the driver's seat. Then concern, as he stepped out of the car and they saw his ripped clothes, the blood and the mud he had been too exhausted to wipe off. They watched him stumble with the weight of it, but not one offered him a glass of water or a ham sandwich. Only Elsie's dad thought he might want to sit down.

It didn't get easier to tell the story, either. It got harder. The sense of relief as he drove out of each driveway was bigger, as was the dread that he would have to start all over again at the next house. His throat was dry and his stomach rumbled, though he was pretty sure he would never be able to eat again.

They were confused, of course. Here in the suburbs, where everything was pastel and perfect, children were lost to college or marriage; they moved away or had their own children who would one day grow up. Occasionally someone else's kids drank or smoked or had an accidental pregnancy. Someone in the next town overdosed a few years ago. How could this happen to their beautiful daughter? Their lovable son? Ordinary children—though theirs were extraordinary, of course, even in their ordinariness—did not turn into monsters. Did not ooze blood and pus on each other. Did not curse and howl and bite their friends. And most of all, they did not hack each other to bits and bury each other in the woods.

The parents were speechless. And then they were not. Then they were too vocal with their disbelief and protests. They called him a liar, they called him a murderer. They accused him of witchcraft, of luring their children away for a weekend of satanic orgies. They cursed him and they blamed him. He knew it was not his fault, but he also knew they saw their children's blood on him, and that was all the proof they needed.

He tried to remind them that this trip had not been his idea—he had just been the driver. He didn't want to say that his were the only parents who would loan them a car. He wanted not to remind them that their children were almost eighteen, and had chosen to go on this weekend getaway of their own accord. He tried not to say it, but sometimes he had too.

Some cried. Some demanded proof. Elsie's dad, who had been so kind with the chair, hit him in the face. He could barely feel it.

When he went home, his parents were out. This was the worst part, or maybe not. He couldn't decide if he wanted company, or never wanted to see anyone again. He turned all the lights on and took a shower, let water steam into his wounds and make him flesh color again. He had to cut the jeans (his favorite pair) off his leg where Marsha had stabbed him with that fire iron. He could barely move his arm from where he had landed when John pushed him down the stairs. There was some unidentifiable substance in his hair. He washed and washed it, but it didn't feel clean. After he got out of the shower, he took his father's electric razor and shaved his head. It hurt. Everything hurt.

He wrapped his clothes in a plastic bag and put them in the outside trash, wearing only a towel. And that's when his parents came home and he had to go through the whole thing again.

161

They took him to the hospital, first. His leg needed nine stitches and a tetanus shot, his arm was broken and his clavicle severely bruised. The doctor didn't even want to talk about the head wound, just set his face in a serious line and swabbed a lot of stinging antiseptic on everything. They gave him extra bandages to take home, and some pretty serious pain pills.

They wanted to keep him overnight, but his parents insisted he come home with them. He was glad. He was especially glad to have someone else taking charge, even if it was only about ordinary things.

On the way to the police station they went to a drive-thru. He took one bite of the burger and threw up all over the car, and then he was sobbing so hard he couldn't even clean himself up, just sat there crying like a baby while his parents mopped up around him, not making eye contact. He found himself apologizing for himself, which was stupid. It was his friends that had all been killed, not theirs. Didn't he have a right to be upset for a while?

At the station, he had to tell the story three more times, then sign a typed version of it. His fingers were stiff when he held the pen. The pain medication was making his head feel woozy, and he hoped he had gotten all the details right. He started to feel like he was watching himself from a great distance, and for some reason this was funny. He couldn't stop laughing. They got him a big drink of water and pulled their chairs a little further away.

He just wanted to go home and go to sleep. Maybe if he woke up in the morning it would be yesterday, all of this would have never happened. But maybe if he let down his guard again, they would get him. He could still hear them on the edge of his brain, growling and mumbling, and that high pitched, screaming laughter.

The police brought in a psychologist. They thought he was crazy, and was it any wonder? The psychologist read his statement and asked him a lot of questions about his feelings, and did he and his friends get along? Was there any jealousy? Problems at home? He answered as best he could, but when they asked about Joey he found he couldn't speak, because there she was behind the psychologist, there she was at the window, there she was scratching at the door, and there she was lying on the ground with his chainsaw where her neck used to be.

There was no air in the room. He couldn't breathe. Were there someone's hands around his throat? The psychologist told him to put his head between his legs and take deep breaths. After a minute the oxygen came rushing back in great gulping breaths and he couldn't stop shaking. The psychologist wanted to send him home, but the police said it was important they get back up to the cabin as soon as possible, just in case there were any survivors.

This, then, was the worst part. Go back? Survivors? Hadn't they been listening to anything he said? If there were survivors, it was bad news for everyone.

They put him in the back of the police cruiser, and to his surprise his parents came along. He sat in between them and let them hold his hands as he concentrated on breathing through his mouth and not throwing up again.

It was a three hour drive, and they had to stop twice so he could be sick. After the second time, his parents let him have the window, and his mother sat in the middle while his father looked out the other side and muttered to himself. His mother tried to stroke his shaven head, but her touch made him jumpy. When they neared the cutoff that lead to

163

the dirt road enough time had passed and he was able to take another pain pill.

The cruiser was better on the unpaved road than his station wagon had been. And they didn't have the radio on, so he didn't have to hear that cheerful weatherman predicting fog and rain or that horrible jingle for Harmon's Hardware. But each tree looked more menacing than the last, and he was sure he was going to pass out when they got to the bridge.

He didn't, but he had to put his head between his legs for a solid fifteen minutes before he could get out of the car. The middle slats were out, just like he had said, and the area around them was still covered with Marsha's blood. He looked down the hole where he had pushed her, but the pills had kicked in and he felt only a curious detachment from it all, and he had to suppress a giggle.

They climbed carefully around the end of the bridge, which was covered in sticks and large rocks. He led them up the footpath, and his tunnel of vision narrowed to a tiny circle. The policewoman asked him if he could stop humming, and he didn't realize he had been. It was the radio jingle for the hardware store.

It was worse the second time. Worse, somehow, to expect it, to not have that playful start, to not have even one kiss, with the promise of something more. To know, right from the beginning, that everything was going to end badly. Worse to hear the bird clock chirping from inside, in the pleasant sunlight, then counting the hours til dawn.

The worst part was that the cabin was just as they had left it. Shouldn't it have changed in some monumental way? Friends had been lost and lives had been shattered, and the front door still hung off its hinges, and the front steps still splintered from where John had chased him back indoors. There was a burnt smell, and smoke still oozed out of the leaves. He felt like it had been years since he'd left this place, but it was only this morning.

He didn't want to go in. Guilt, fear, shame, and sadness all stabbed away at his insides with equal insistence. He was walking over their footprints from twenty four hours ago, when they were innocent, happy, alive. When they were human.

He could see the blood on the inside of the bedroom window. Elsie's window, where John had found her; dragging herself by her nails across the wood plank floor. So there was some of John's blood as well, but not as much. Most of that was in the cellar. Another place he didn't want to go.

When the male police officer drew his gun at the rustle in the leaves and the female officer put her arm out to stop them from going any closer, that was the worst part, because he'd heard where the rustle was coming from. He knew what, and who, was there.

The male officer shouted at the shifting leaves. He told them to freeze, to drop their weapons, to stand up slowly. For a moment no one moved, or breathed, except the thing in the leaves. The officer called one last warning, then fired. There was a cry, and a moan, and he was on his knees with his hands over his head, saying her name over and over again, while his mother tried to touch him, to comfort him, but he couldn't bear it.

After it was quiet again and he could look up, he saw the officer who had shot at her poking gently through the foliage. He scuffed some aside with his foot and picked up his kill—a small yellow fox, its bright

165

color not the same as Joey's hair after all. Then he yelped and dropped it, and the other officer began speaking to someone on her shoulder radio. His mother tried to block his view, but not before he'd seen Joey's severed hand in the foxes' mouth, still wearing the ring he'd bought her.

It was good the fox had been killed, he thought. Would whatever had infected Joey have otherwise spread to the animal? He wondered where Marsha's body had ended up. Hopefully somewhere no scavenger could eat it.

The officers began moving towards the cabin, weapons drawn, crouching like cats. He heard one cry out at the sight of John in the doorway, and someone else weeping. To his surprise, it was his father, who had just glimpsed Joey's ruined face through the leaves.

That might have been the worst part, seeing his father cry. Funny, but it had never occurred to him that his father could cry. He couldn't watch, but he couldn't look away. He couldn't remember the last time he had seen another man cry. John had shed tears of blood before he was beheaded, but it wasn't really the same thing at all. His mother took his father's hand and they stood there together, looking at the cabin instead of him.

The worst part was when the police came out of the cabin and confirmed everything he had told them. The worst part was that he hadn't imagined it, hadn't dreamed it, wasn't crazy. The worst part was that they were all gone, and he had killed them.

People started arriving, in uniforms and white suits. He sat on a stump and watched them put bloodstained twigs in plastic bags, carry things in and out of the cabin, their white gloves turning crimson. He wanted to ask someone if he could have Joey's ring.

166

When the ambulance came it was slow and quiet. They scuffed up the leaves and put Joey in a large black bag with a zipper on top. Then they went into the cabin and came out with two more. He told them about Marsha and the female office talked into her shoulder again, requesting someone look into it. Drag the river, maybe. Whatever it took.

The sun started to set, and somehow that wasn't the worst part. He felt both panic and relief as he heard the Carolina Wren chime seven o'clock from inside the cabin. Maybe everyone here would start to drip and ooze and everything would be finished for good. Or maybe it would be time to go home. He found he was curiously satisfied with both options. When another hour had passed and the Eastern Bluebird sang into the fading light, he took one of the doctor's pills. The clearing around the cabin was quiet and he realized he had never heard a real bird sing, only the clock. He suddenly wanted to smash it.

The original two officers who had driven them began to get nervous, and he realized they were taking him seriously. No one was doubting his story anymore, and so just in case, everyone began to pack up their equipment. They would return tomorrow, but told him he didn't have to come. Behind him, his parents breathed an audible sigh of relief.

On the ride home, he didn't feel sick. He watched the stars out the window, and kept an eye out for anything jumping out from the darkness. He had stolen a scalpel from a medical examiner and felt he could take on anything. When he fell asleep and dreamed of Joey, coming at him with that smile, he woke up screaming and the driver almost swerved into a tree.

167

Wouldn't that be ironic? To have made it through all this and then die in the woods after all. Was that irony? He was so tired he could no longer be sure.

It was well after midnight when they made it home, though their house had no bird clock to tell them, only regular ones that ticked. He tried to go to bed but found the darkness smothered him like a body bag, and watched infomercials until dawn.

The worst part was calling the owner of the cabin and asking for his deposit back. He didn't get it, of course. The property had been all but destroyed, and the owner was unwilling to chalk it up to anything but normal teen behavior. He thought about telling the police, but decided he wanted it all to be over more than he wanted his seventy five bucks back.

They told him he had to go to counseling. He got to miss school, but what was the point? The counselor didn't have any useful advice; didn't have anything to relate it to. He read some books on familicide and the Holocaust, but the photo essays made him feel weak. He might have preferred social studies to this.

He sat by the door most nights with a hammer or something heavy by his hand, just in case. When it turned light out he took the pills the new doctor prescribed, the ones that were supposed to help him sleep, but when he dozed off he only got disjointed nightmares and terrible headaches. He fell somewhere between consciousness and sleep. Sometimes he sleepwalked. Once he awoke to a loud noise, only to find he had dropped the hammer on his foot and couldn't even feel it.

His arm healed, and his hair grew back. He graduated in the spring,

168

despite having barely participated in his classes. He walked with a slight limp when he bothered to walk at all. Mostly he sat by the door, watching his parents go in and out, watching his classmates go off to college, or to start families, or to make their own, menial, mistakes. He grew older.

This, then, was the worst part. Not the woods, or the blood, or the long car ride home. Not Joey's face or Marsha's missing body. Not the police, the physiologists, the pills or the nightmares.

The worse part was surviving.

For A Good Time

The line rang seven times, and my hand holding the phone started to sweat; not pooling in beads like during a workout but an oozy, unattractive dampness. I thought of swamps and mildews, mushrooms and public speaking. Finally, someone answered.

"Hello?" The voice was uncertain, high pitched for a man but low for a woman. I was stumped into silence.

"Hello?" said the voice again, "Who is this?"

"Um," I said back. My voice squeaked. I cleared my throat and tried again. "I'm, uh, looking for a good time?"

My new friend laughed. It was melodic and genuine, but gave me to clue as to the gender. I had assumed it would be female, but why? All of the women I knew had better things to do than sneak into men's restrooms and write their phone numbers on the wall.

"Are you?" He or she said.

"I found, I uh, found your number in this bathroom on 5th street—" I traced the figure with the tip of my finger. It wasn't just written, it was carved into the plaster. Whoever was on the other end of the phone wanted to make sure the good time didn't get away from them.

"Oh hon," said the voice, "that's because I put it there!" She (maybe) chuckled, and it was surprisingly warm and friendly. I almost hung up, but I was too curious.

"Who are you?" and then, because I'd been teetering on the verge of tipsy all night, "What kind of person goes around putting their real phone number on the bathroom wall?"

"What kind of person calls it?" he (possibly) fired back.

"Okay." I said. "Touche."

"I'm Kel." said the voice.

"That's not a name," I told it, "That's a syllable."

"Mister," she said, "If you called me up just to be rude to me, I am not interested. I'm hanging up now."

"Wait!" I said, though I couldn't for the life of me imagine why. "Don't go."

He relented.

"Okay." I pictured him as an old-timey psychiatrist, crossing one leg over the other as I lay on his couch. "Tell me about yourself."

I wondered if this was what it was like calling a phone sex hotline. I felt dirty. Freud had been a psychiatrist, hadn't he? He'd always had a pointed little beard in the pictures I'd seen. I wondered if the face that belonged to my companion had a little beard like that.

"I'm Gary."

"Is that your real name?" Kel asked. It was, but I didn't want this monosyllabic stranger to know that I was stupid enough to give out real information. What was next, my credit card and social security number? A home address?

"What's it to you?" I asked.

"You called me," Kel said again. I pictured a big boned woman with long blonde hair. Tanned but not orange. Pleasantly muscular and a little plump.

"How long ago did you leave your number here?"

"2002," said the good time girl. "I've got surprisingly few calls since then."

"Really?" I asked, not sure if it was a question, "Can I ask you why you wrote it there?"

I pictured her shrugging into the phone.

"I was younger and stupider. It seemed like a good way to meet men. To get noticed." I undressed her in my mind. She was wearing a

171

white tennis dress, practical underwear. Ankle socks.

"Did it work?"

"I met you, didn't I?" She laughed again, and it was lower, more masculine. My mind's eye refocused and I saw a thin man with a Freddy Mercury mustache.

He was still talking.

"I used to get one or two calls a year, but it's been a while. I was starting to think they'd renovated."

"Nope," I said, mouth dry, "It's still here."

"Are the walls still that horrible blue?"

I looked around as though maybe they had changed since I'd come in, but they were still a washed out eggshell blue, flecked with steel gray where the enamel had chipped.

"Still blue," I told him, "My girlfriend says the ladies' room is the same, only pink, like Pepto Bismal."

"Your girlfriend?" he was laughing now, again and again. I realized my mistake. "Honey, why are you calling strangers in the public toilet when your girlfriend is out there waiting for you? Is she out there?"

I pictured Nancy in her new dress, playing with her french fries while she waited for me to come back from the restroom.

"I lied," I told Kel, face burning, "There's no girlfriend."

"What's her name?" he asked, gently, mustache blooming into a swarthy goatee, the kind my modern history professor sported in college. I pictured Kel in one of Dr. Mishou's sport coats, endlessly clearing his throat and putting up new slides.

"Nance." I said. "Nancy."

"Nancy and Gary," Kel purred, like an old time movie star, "How sweet. Rhyming couplets."

"We're having, ah, some problems." I had a sudden urge for a

172

cigarette, though I'd quit years ago.

"Bedroom?" asked Kel, "Erectile? You or her? Both? They make a pill for that."

"It's complicated." I said. "Family stuff."

"Pregnancy scare? Condom malfunction? Bossy in-laws? Yours or hers?" Kel's rapid fire questions were making me feel winded.

"No, nothing like that." I didn't want to talk about Arthur Reyes or my accusations, or the trip we'd planned together but now couldn't afford.

"You ungracious bastard." Kel's voice was still light, but I pictured a Disney villain, like Ursuala, tentacles swirling and suckers snapping. "Go tell your girlfriend you love her. Hang up on little old me and get off the pot. Or better yet, hand the phone to her. She deserves better than you, and there's a lot of other guys out there."

There was a moment of silence, and I spun the roll of paper back and forth, letting it creep a little closer to the floor with every twirl before switching directions and sucking it back up into the dispenser.

"Unless," said Kel, "You really are after that good time."

"I, uh—" I couldn't think of anything to say. I considered longingly my glass of water out at the table across from Nance, or better yet, my gin and tonic.

"You want a blow job, pretty boy?" Kel cooed, temptress like. "Want to come over to my place and let me run you ragged? Or we can do this over the phone, my talking and you just listening, all hands and no dance, you know what I mean? Just squirt your load all over my number when it's time. Give me a little something to remember you by." She coughed, and I sat on the toiled lid, frozen, transfixed.

"It's been done before," said Kel when the coughing subsided.

"Really?" I whispered, voice caught again.

173

Kel laughed, and I could hear a smile through the phone.

"Maybe."

"Have you—" I rolled my tongue around in my mouth. It was like a dry sponge, dead weight in the cargo hold of my mouth. "Have you been back here since you wrote it?" I said it like it was a dirty secret, like graffiti art pornography instead of ten little numbers which I hadn't heard combined like this before twenty minutes ago.

"No," he said calmly, and his hair lengthened, beatnik style. "That night was not a good experience for me. Maybe that's why I wrote it." Now we were talking about a poem, a rousing political piece, an award winning play. "Maybe I just wanted to see if I could."

"You could," I said, awkwardly feeling the need to praise, to reassure, "You did. Congratulations."

There was silence again, and a noise I couldn't identify.

"Gary," he said, "Can I tell you something?"

"Okay." I leaned my back against the wall, drew my feet up onto the lid so my heels rested against my buttocks. Someone came in and went to the sink. I ignored him.

"I'm glad I did it. But a little part of me—just the tiniest hidden baby piece—wishes it never happened."

"Why's that?" He had a beaked nose, maybe some little silver glasses.

"I feel vulnerable. Too exposed."

"You could change your number." Blue eyes, the color of the bathroom wall.

"I suppose I could. But what if he calls?"

"He who?" I poked at the paint, chipping it.

"He whoever. Him. You know, 'the one.'"

"I don't know." I said. I'd been in so long I found I needed to

174

relieve my bladder again. I stood up and lifted the lid.

"You don't, I guess." Kel sighed. "You've got Nance. You're not the one."

I pissed into the bowl and wondered if Kel could hear it on the other end.

"I might be the one," I said, "You never know."

"You're not." She said. "Probably. Unless you want to meet up? Figure it out in person?" She had long dark hair and almond skin, a slinky black dress and lace lingerie. A femme fatale with a dangerous looking cigarette holder.

My hands felt clammy again, and my penis shrunk in my hand in fear as I tucked it back away.

"Probably not a good idea," I said, trying to sound gentle and not broadcast my nervousness. What had I done? I'd told this stranger my—our—names and location. He could come down here at any moment and I'd never even know it. Not to mention the discomfort the idea of a sexual rendezvous with someone I wasn't even sure the sex of gave me. I suddenly wanted to be with Nancy very badly. I flushed the toilet.

"What was that?" asked Kel, still uncomfortably close to my ear. "Are you flushing? Are you flushing me?"

"Sorry," I said, praying a little that this would not come back to bite me.

"They always flush me," he sighed again, shrinking and widening, a sad middle aged man alone in his studio apartment. "Every last stinkin' one of them."

"I've got to go," I told him, zipping myself back up.

"You men," she said, but there was no malice in her voice. "You're all alike." Did her eyes sparkle just a bit? Was she teasing me?

175

"Okay," I said, suddenly tired of this game, wanting real life back, wanting Nance and my burger and my drink. "I guess. Sorry. Bye."

"Hey Gary," I heard her say as I was closing the phone, slipping the lock of the stall, trying to forget those ten digits burning into my brain, "Did you have a good time?"

Bones

After Ben died, Cammie had watched Lindsay Fifty at the playground, laughing with her friends. She sat in the shadows of the big oak tree in her hand-me-down clothes and drank in the sight of Lindsay Fifty in her shiny new jumper and she ached to be her. It was not that Lindsay Fifty was particularly pretty. She was not particularly smart, or even particularly interesting. She was, in fact, shallow, simple, and spoiled; an only child pampered by two caring but distant parents, obsessed with the superficialities of money and appearance.

But right then, it didn't matter. Starting that summer she had wanted to be Lindsay Fifty for the pure and simple reason that Lindsay Fifty was utterly and completely ordinary. Her life was simple, arranged, predetermined. It held no surprises. They weren't allowed.

While every day Lindsay Fifty giggled with her identical friends and went home to eat dinner with her parents, Cammie lived in silence. Her parents' tiny house, which had once been filled with light brighter than any of Lindsay Fifty's sequins, was now dark and silent. The shades were always pulled down tightly to the window pane, and there was no longer the sound of babies' laughter or mother's singing. Ben, who had been better than any shiny dress, any number of silvery friends, was gone. He was her father's smile, her mother's reason to get up in the morning. And now Ben was dead, and Mother wouldn't come out of her bedroom. Father wouldn't come home from working until it was too dark to see. He refused to light a lantern, but would pull aside the curtains and sit all alone in the gloom and eat his dinner. Sometimes, Cammie would sneak out of bed to watch him. Once he caught her; the full moon made her hair glow, giving her away.

"Come here." he said. His voice was gravely and soft. Obediently, she came a little closer.

"Closer." He beckoned to her. His features shone in the moonlight. His voice was a little louder, a little harsher. She took another step and suddenly he pushed his chair over and lunged at her—grabbing her up in his arms and holding her tight, burying his face in her moon-glowing hair and mumbling words she couldn't make out. She stayed completely still, unsure how to react. She was really too big to be picked up, and even when she was smaller her father rarely touched her. After a moment he put her down and pushed her away. His face was wet and it glistened sharply.

"I'm sorry," he whispered, and she didn't ask for what.

It was another year before she found the bones. It was a bright sunny day, and for the first time since Ben's death, she opened the kitchen curtains to the daylight. For the first time since Ben's death, the kitchen saw light stronger than moonlight, and it was not sure how to react. It showed the dust and grime, and the neglect of nearly two years of housework. Insects which had taken to enjoying discarded scraps in a peaceful dark ran for cover under the furniture and old food boxes which had piled up. For the first time since Ben's death, Cammie tied up her hair and picked up a mess.

Most of the boxes were empty. They were crates of wood or cardboard that had once held fresh fruit and vegetables. In a nondescript cardboard box towards the middle of the stack, Cammie found the bones. They were small and whitish, varying from the size of a fingernail to about a foot long. There was no skull. She started and flung the box away from her, spilling its contents out onto the dusty floor. The bones clattered loudly in the quiet, and she heard her mother stirring in the locked master bedroom. She picked them up as quickly as she could, shoving the brittle sticks back into their paper coffin. She didn't know who they belonged to, and she was almost afraid to find out. She was sure Lindsay Fifty didn't find boxes of bones in her families' kitchen.

That night, she left the box of bones on the newly clean table for her father to see.

"Cammie." He was knocking on her door. It was dark, there was no moon. She hadn't been into the kitchen at night for months. But he was knocking.

"Cammie." He opened her door and came in, and for some reason she was absolutely terrified. No one besides her had been inside that room since the death of baby Ben.

Father sat on the edge of her bed and stared at her. She drew her legs up under the blanket, and scooted as far away from him as possible.

"It's not what you think," he said, "Those aren't your brother's bones."

She didn't know whether or not to believe him, but in the end it didn't matter. Word somehow got out. Word always got out. Sooner or later, all her classmates knew that Cammie's little brother's bones were kept in a box in the kitchen. Sooner or later, everyone knew. But no one asked. They just stopped speaking to her, stopped speaking at her or around her, or even about her. The closest she got to the others was when she watched Lindsay Fifty and her friends talk in the yard. By the time school let out for the summer, Cammie had not seen her mother in two years. Her father came home from work even later, leaving his daughter alone in the company of a locked bedroom door and a lonely box of bones. Alone every night in the dark, Cammie dreamed of living

179

the ignorant, uncomplicated life of Lindsay Fifty.

And then the circus came to town.

Mister Zimitri's Big Top Circus! was garish and disgusting. It was
cheap and decadent, and people for miles around paid a dollar for the
big top tent and fifty cents for the sideshow. The sideshow. The parade
of freaks. Overly bright sandwich boards told tales of the Sad Clown,
the Invisible Woman, the Boneless Wonder, the Two-Headed Man.
There were midgets, a Fat Lady, the Living Torso, the Wolf Boy, the
Four-Legged Child—it seemed freaks from every part of the world had
congregated in one place, earning fifty cents after fifty cents, enduring
hungry eyes and grotesque insults. Cammie stole a dollar from her
father to see it twice.

The tent was dank and humid, smelling of sweat and urine. Calliope
music tinkled faintly in the background. The crowd pressed together,
undulating as one towards the platform up front. Cammie watched in
awe, barely blinking, as the Fat Lady waddled onstage and danced, her
mammoth rolls convoluting sickeningly over her skintight costume.
The Wolf Boy, covered in fur, scampered around—first on all fours,
then on two legs—barking like a dog. And the Boneless Wonder—a
tall thin girl made of silver who tied her body in knots—she caught
Cammie's eye and smiled at her, smiled in a way that suggested she
knew all about the contents of the box, and in fact, those were her
bones, and Father was only keeping them safe until she needed them
again. For the finale, the midgets made a pyramid of their bodies, and
the Two-Headed Man carried the Limbless Wonder out and placed him
on the top. The Sad Clown cavorted around them, and the Limbless
Wonder wobbled to and fro, grinning happily at the fascinated crowd,
but Cammie was barely watching. She was thinking of the silver girl—

the Boneless Wonder. She was thinking of her eyes and her smile.

She had to get out of the tent, had to get out of this claustrophobic prison. Her head swam and she felt nauseous, but she couldn't push her way back through the crowd—they were pushing against her towards the freaks—they were shouting at them—calling them names and throwing bottles and peanuts and spitting at their retreating figures. The world grew blurry and out of focus, and then suddenly she was out—taking great gasps of air and sunlight and trying to quiet her head and her stomach, but it was too much, and she vomited a messy pile next to the sideshow tent. Then she wandered a little ways away, to a place where the grass was still long, untrampled by eager feet. She sat down and took out her remaining fifty cents and looked at it. She couldn't go back in there, could she? In the end, she put the coins back in her pocket and lay down, letting the grass cover her body.

When she woke up, it was to the sound of a man's voice and the sight of a few pale stars far above her.

"Last call!" the voice was shouting, "Last show! This is your last chance to see Mister Zimitri's Big Top Circus! Hurry and get your tickets! Half price! Last call!"

Cammie sat up, and saw the shadow of the carnival barker, his top hat making its shape bizarrely irregular. She traded the barker for a yellow paper ticket, and stepped inside the bigtop tent. Where the freak's tent had been hot and humid, the big top was cool and arid. Above, trapeze artists whirled. Below, tigers jumped through hoops and elephants let people ride them. It was a magical, eerie world. The crowd tittered nervously, unsure if it was all right to laugh and cheer for something so strange and surreal. The Freaks had had a label—the crowd knew it was allowed, and even expected, for them to boo the parade. But Mister Zimitri's Big Top Circus! was unfamiliar territory.

Cammie sat without moving, even after the show was over and the rest of the crowd had left, her hand clutching the worn wooden seat beside her. She watched as the barker and two mimes began to sweep the ring in the middle smooth again, flattening the footprints and skid marks out of the sawdust and dirt. She walked outside and saw the four midgets from the freak show smoking cigarettes, their faces shining redly from the lit ends. The white tubes reminded her of bones, and she walked home quickly over the fields, arriving back even later than her father.

The next day she was there again, and the day after that. She had no more money, and so she stood outside the smaller tent, watching through the flap whenever anyone went in or out. It was hard to see, but not impossible. After a while, she got the idea to go around the back of the tent, and watch the freaks when they entered and exited. They were between shows, and there was only one there. The Boneless Wonder. She had a can of silver paint and a brush, and was touching up the places the color had rubbed off. She looked up and caught Cammie's eyes again.

"C'mere kid," her voice was surprisingly ordinary. She handed Cammie the paintbrush. "Give me a hand."

Cammie dipped the bristle delicately into the can, and ran the silver sheen over the Boneless Wonder's shoulders.

"I'm Cammie." she said.

"S'ree." said the silver girl. She closed her eyes and let Cammie paint her eyelids and the bridge of her nose.

"So what's your story?" Her beautiful green eyes sprung open so suddenly that Cammie fumbled and nearly dropped the paintbrush. An

182

orb of silver fell to the ground, staining the grass below it.

"Your story," prompted S'ree. "Are you a freak too?"

"My father has a box of bones that belong to my brother." It came out in a rush. It was the first time she'd ever spoken it aloud. The paintbrush dripped onto her foot.

"How do you know?" It came from the Fat Lady. The freaks had formed a semi-circle behind her as she painted. "How do you know they aren't bones from a chicken or a dog?"

"I don't." said Cammie. The Fat Lady just nodded.

"I'm Minnie." she stuck out her hand. Cammie shook it. It was like shaking anyone else's hand, there was just more of it. She was no more freak than anyone else.

For one night, she was normal again. For one night, she could stop wishing for the life of Lindsay Fifty. Lindsay Fifty would never have had a night like this. Lindsay Fifty didn't have a box of bones—but she also didn't have any real friends. She couldn't talk to the Wolf Boy and the Two-Headed Man, or paint the skin of a Boneless Wonder. She would never breath in the smoke from a midget's cigarette, or learn that the Invisible Woman was only shy, the Sad Clown just a little lonely. Lindsay Fifty would not have known what to do when introduced to a Living Torso.

"I'm Dave." he said. He didn't have a hand to shake, so she just nodded. When you're a girl with a box of bones in your kitchen, greeting a man with no limbs is not a challenge. And when your body is only a torso, a girl with a curious past is nothing so extraordinary.

Scatter, Safely Crossing

Apparently, Doug's mother had not been honoring his final wishes and had been keeping his remains in what was basically a bedazzled coffee can on her shelf of knickknacks. The woman who would have been my mother-in-law, had that truck not hit the Huntington corner stop too fast on an icy night, had finally broken down and agreed to have his ashes scattered on the Little League field where he had played as a boy.

All this time, I thought blankly when I finally found out, *all this time*. There was no end to this thought, as though my brain, unable to process this new information, had simply short circuited midway through. All I could imagine from the moment I heard was Doug's spirit, or whatever it was, wanting to roam free and play baseball forever but instead trapped beside his mother, watching her cooking shows and listening to her phone arguments with her sisters, stuck in a world of glitter glue and hair products instead of fertilizing the outfield. I didn't have the energy to be angry, or to question why it had taken her twelve months to call Dan or myself. I just wanted it to be over.

The plan was for the two of us to drive from my apartment to the green Missouri diamond that would be Doug's final resting place. My car was old and sometimes terrifyingly unstable; Dan would pick me up and we would drive the day long journey together, back to their hometown where both their families still lived. We could have flown, but the drive seemed more important to both of us; an homage, a token, a penance.

We hadn't had any contact since the funeral, where we had sat together without speaking, numb with exhaustion and horror and scarcely able to register the other's presence. I couldn't remember if he'd cried. I could hardly remember if I had. We had hugged goodbye, barely touching, barely making contact, and I hadn't seen him since. He was like an estranged relative, brother being perhaps too close an illustration, but I didn't have another synonym, another way to describe this final connection to Doug, to what could have been. We had never been real friends, had never had anything in common besides Doug, but it had been enough. Without him we would struggle with smalltalk and depth in equal measures. My tongue was thick in my mouth. I had no words for anything.

Dan would wrap the trip into a visit with his parents and his childhood, while I would fly back home after scattering the ashes into the sticky wind. Doug's mother did not want to be present, did not want to see her son's best friend and girlfriend, perhaps wanted to deny that the past had ever taken place. She had already mailed the makeshift urn to Dan's parent's address, and now that it was out of her kitchen she was free to ignore its existence, numbing herself with Franzia and daytime talk shows, iced white wine and paternity tests. I would never give her grandchildren or run her daytime errands. Maury Povitch was closer to her than I could now ever be.

Dan's mother loved her knickknacks even more than Doug's did. The two women had what they referred to as "front parlors" overflowing with Matreshka dolls and Japanese chess sets and ornate Vietnamese pottery. Doug's was particularly fond of craft show fare, whereas Dan's was more tasteful, primarily made up of the Greek memorabilia that reminded her of her family. She claimed she was descended from gypsy royalty and a love of trinkets ran in her veins, which sounded racist but plausible. I often wondered if the familiar clutter of each other's homes had been what had drawn Doug and Dan to each other as

185

children; if subconsciously neither had felt entirely comfortable in a place without plaster and button eyes on them at all times.

It was early spring on the day we left, and the further south we got the hotter the sun became. It had been a wet winter and I could already feel a hint of summer edging on. I had visited Doug's family here in the thick of August, with the unrelenting heat and the cicadas as loud as a freeway, when the sky was muggy and sodden with no escape that was not air conditioned frigidity. I hoped it would be clear when we scattered Doug so his ashes could fly free instead of dampening to mud. I hoped he was thinking of me, wherever he was. I hoped he was watching this road trip we had committed to and smiling at its' clumsiness.

We stopped and had barbecue for lunch, the fatty meat sitting heavy in my stomach and making me sweat. Dan drank two glasses of sweet tea and told me about his new job. I had a Pepsi and felt the sugar coat my teeth, wished my toothbrush wasn't packed so deeply in my duffel bag.

Dan had crooked teeth, but charming like a British movie star's rather than a snaggletoothed villain in a B horror movie. I watched them as he talked, and even as he chewed, eventually putting my sunglasses on so he couldn't see me staring. I wondered if he brushed them more regularly than Doug had, Doug who relied on a regime comprised mostly of toothpicks and mouthwash and used to laugh at me for brushing and flossing so diligently. When he died, he hadn't been to the dentist in two years.

As we paid our tab and changed CDs I wondered if I had taken Dan's presence in my life for granted. It was occurring to me now how many vital moments and holidays he had been a part of, seemingly

186

without me even noticing. What if this was the last time I saw him? What if, without Doug to hold this mini family together, we would drift apart to our different corners of the world? Would it be like losing Doug a second time, or would it fade off in the distance the way my own childhood memories had?

The sun set golden in the west, taking with it the blossoming heat. We drove on in silence, and I convinced myself it was a companionable silence, that it was okay to sit and not talk, that that's what one did with friends, with family. By eight o'clock we had been traveling for twelve hours and neither one of us had mentioned Doug.

Around ten, Dan pulled over and let me drive. He wasn't much taller than me but I still had to pull the seat forward what felt like miles. He fell asleep almost as soon as we switched places and I turned the music off when my head began to buzz with constant noise. Dan breathed so softly I could barely hear it above the engine and when I snuck a peek at him the lights of passing signs dappled his face and neck. I felt drunk with exhaustion, my brain spinning and wheeling and unable to land a single thought.

I turned on the news and heard a story about a war on foreign soil and all the hardships the deaths of their husbands was causing the local women, a biography about a film composer who had just died, and a puff piece about a goat who had chased a twelve year old up a tree. In only a few hours we would be there, and I felt inexplicably nervous.

Doug and I had met at work, the lamest introductory story of all of our friends. We both had entry level jobs in the same building, he as a glorified errand boy, me in data entry. We bonded over our shared hatred of the office manager, a stern and skeletal woman with hair

187

pulled back so tight it made my skin hurt to look at her. We spent most of our time instant messaging each other and both quit within a year, never sure if we should use the office manager as a reference.

Dan woke up as we crossed the border and wanted to drive again. He turned the music back to the same mix of soundalikes that had been playing for the past day, hummed along tunelessly. I felt hyper alert and scanned the road for wildlife as we turned off the interstate and onto an unlit single lane highway. I rolled down the window and let the sounds of the south wash over me.

"I love that," said Dan, his voice an air punch in the darkness, "I can't sleep when it's quiet. I feel like I never realize it til I'm home."

It brought a lump to my throat, and I thought for an irrational second that I actually might start to cry. My family was scattered across the country, my parents no longer living in the place where I had grown up. Maybe it was this grown man who still called that house full of china dolls and unused place settings "home," maybe it was only the lateness of the hour and the emotional exhaustion of the trip, but I wanted to take his hand, to let him know that I understood, somewhere deep inside me, but I didn't and the moment was gone. We pushed through the night and into morning.

We stopped at a gas station only thirty miles from town. While Dan refueled I went inside to buy us drinks and stretch my legs. I felt jittery and a little sick, the product of a day of meals made up of junk food and caffeine. I bought a bottle of water and couldn't stop drinking it, nervous little sips like a bird at a fountain.

I climbed back into the truck cab and my body was so sore from sitting the skin felt nearly numb. I gave him his drink and he thanked me, I felt flustered and thanked him for driving. He said "no problem" like maybe it really wasn't, like we were just on this casual road trip with a non-traumatic destination. I asked him how his parents were and he said fine, still going, the usual. He turned the GPS off and it looked like he could have driven these streets blindfolded.

We pulled into the driveway of his parent's house, a neat but rundown neighborhood like all the other neat but rundown neighborhoods in this town. The house was dark and sleepy.

"They're gone until the morning," he said. "I'll get you set up in my brother's old room."

The truck stopped with finality, but I felt like I was still moving, had switched from land legs to sea legs. We stumbled out into the buzzing night carrying our few bags. Dan found me a towel, a pillow; I hunted out my hidden toothbrush and cleaned my teeth. The house was so quiet after the car ride that my ears were ringing. I felt wide awake, as though I'd passed through tired to the other side.

"Want a drink?" Dan called from a few rooms away, farther than it seemed he had ever been, "There's a couple of beers in here."

I followed the sound of his voice down the hall to the kitchen, where he stood in sock feet in front of a fridge covered in magnets from all fifty states. On the other side of the room I could dimly see a hundred plastic eyes staring at me from a shelf above a Saran-wrapped couch.

"Where is he?" I asked. I couldn't say his name. My mouth was dry, suddenly parched and arid despite the variety of sodas I had consumed throughout the day. I reached for the beer Dan was holding out without really looking at it. My heart was beating enormously hard, I could hear it on the inside of my head.

I flipped on the light switch in the front room and searched for the

189

urn Doug's mother had sent. There was so much to look at my eyes got overwhelmed.

"It's not there." Dan ushered me out of the room, turned the light off behind me, showed me a lumpy package addressed to him, care of his parents.

"Don't open it," I said, a little claustrophobic, a little nauseous. "Can we go outside?"

Dan nodded and led the way, gently putting the package down on the dining room table before opening the door. Outside was a wonderful wraparound porch, about as far away from the knickknacks as you could get. It was huge and breezy and surprisingly empty of clutter. I took deep breaths until my heart slowed.

Doug and I had a spot we went to on weekend mornings, sometimes a little hungover, sometimes early in the day before going out of town. It was only a few blocks from our apartment and the middle aged waitress knew our names, asked about us kindly and sometimes gave us free coffees. The food was nothing special but the service was fast and the portions were large and they served tomatillo salsa with nearly everything. Doug loved tomatillo salsa.

The air outside was cool but the breeze that stirred my hair was warm. I leaned on the railing and drank my beer. The taste was slightly metallic and it felt good to stand.

"What time's your flight?" Dan angled next to me and I could feel the heat of him through the fabric of my shirt.

"Four," I said. Just enough time to do what I came to and not hang around. This was Doug's home, not mine. There was no one else here I needed to see, nothing to do besides the obvious.

Doug had a tattoo, a tiny patch of stripes on his upper right hip that looked like claws had raked this singular portion of his skin, leaving inky scars on their way by. Doug, an armchair animal rights activist, said it was in solidarity with all of the extinct species we would never see again, and besides, it looked really cool. I liked to put my hand against it, match each fingertip to the point of the claw, trace the outline of the space the tiger paw would have touched.

"I guess I'll turn in," said Dan, but he didn't move, just stood there looking at the trees in the back yard, fast rooted with stars towering bright above them. I closed my eyes and breathed in deeply again, sucking down great lungfuls of air that smelled somehow alive, like it could sprout leaves at any moment.

Doug didn't really have an accent, except when he was on the phone with his mother. He told me once he had worked hard to get rid of it, thought it would hold him back in job interviews, stop him from being taken seriously.

Dan and I stood up to go inside at the same time.
"Ladies first," he said, scooting backwards and letting me by. I struggled with the sliding door and he leaned over to help me, reassuring me it always stuck from this side, wiggling it a few times until it opened with a whir.

Doug's eyes would crinkle when he smiled. I called him "Old Man Eyes" and told him he would have crow's feet in a few years, and laugh lines, and a furrow between his eyebrows from thinking so hard, staring at the computer as he answered e-mails and read the news and played a game. Someday he would have been a real old man, with reading glasses and paper skin and shoes with non-slip soles. We could have laughed together about his youth, when even then his hands were dry and his hair had a mind of its own, wild and untamable, now extinct like the Tasmanian tiger that might have marked his flesh.

An eddy of artificially cool air washed out to mingle with the night and I shivered involuntarily. Dan put a hand on the base of my neck and he was warm, so warm, but I froze still and the night froze with me and we stood like statues, a portrait of sorrow and heartache and longing and loss, until the spell broke with the heart hammering squawk of a frog somewhere in the mire and I turned to Dan and pulled him close to me, my undrunk beer sloshing at the bottom of the bottle like a wave.

Dan was not a hugger, but the first time I'd met him and had held out a hand to shake, he bypassed it and put his arms around me instead.

"We're family now," he'd said.

Dan's sweater was rough against my face but it felt so good to hold someone, anyone, that I was unable to let go, even after his other arm circled and rested around me, even after it released, I was lost, I was gone somewhere into the fabric of his clothing and the air and the night and my memories sealed away for the last twelve months in a place other than here.

"Hey," he said. He was gentle but firm as he pried my arms away and held me steady while my eyes could only focus on something unseen in the dark behind him.

"Hey," he said again, "look at me." He didn't say "It's going to be okay," because it wasn't, obviously, nothing was ever going to be okay again so I didn't say it either, and the night enveloped us with its blackness, pushing us together until it felt inevitable, cosmic, simple, for our mouths to stumble and catch upon each other, over and over again and nothing like the wispy embrace we had exchanged at the funeral, nothing like the weak side by side we had shared for the last day and a half; it was like drowning, it was like breathing, it was like finally sleeping after a year of broken dreams and gritty eyes and pale, watery dawns.

I slipped my hands beneath his scratchy sweater and his skin was soft and alive. I touched his hair and it was light and downy, silkier than I had expected, free of tangles as I drew my fingers through. He was darker than Doug, shorter and more compact, but still somehow familiar. He pulled off my shirt and this time the mix of air felt like a caress. His hands skimmed my back, my shoulders, and finally my breasts, but hesitantly, and I heard his breath hitch like a sob, but he didn't stop, and I didn't want him to.

He crushed me back into the porch railing, and what I felt was strange relief. The wood dug into my lower back as my brain gave in and my body took over and we were all hands and mouths and skin on skin, silent and desperate and seeking oblivion like Doug's mother at the bottom of a bottle. Once I thought I heard him breathe my name, but it might have been only the whisper of grass in the wind.

I pulled back there were tears on his cheeks, and when I kissed them away they evaporated on my lips like rain and he took my hand and pulled me into the house, down the hall and to a different bedroom from the one that held my suitcase. He slid my jeans down over my hips like he had done it a thousand times before, guiding me down onto his childhood bed to lay beside him, face to face, shifting his weight as we together removed the rest of his clothes. His back was lightly damp, his face was damper. I couldn't stop running my hands along his skin, couldn't get over the novelty of having someone close to me.

He was hard against my leg and I wanted him, needed him so badly I could hardly form another thought in my head, couldn't even force the words past my broken lips.

"Shit," said Dan, "I don't have a condom." My mind was blank, I could barely remember condoms, I hadn't been on the pill for months, hadn't had a reason to be.

"Hang on a sec," Dan opened the door and left the room. I turned the light off, suddenly self-conscious. He returned in a moment with a crinkle of foil.

"It's my dad's," he said, "his secret stash. I found them when I was a teenager, never used one before."

"Don't worry," he said, "They're not that old."

I laid back and he slid against me and as soon as I felt him inside me I started to cry.

He stilled immediately, but I told him it was okay, and maybe it was, finally, or would be, someday. I felt myself opening and closing to him like a mollusk, like a sob, everything laid bare and vulnerable like a tiny piece of oyster meat. We moved together, alone at last though involuntarily, and Doug evaporated from between us, just this once.

When I awoke the sky was bright and the cicadas had gone to bed. Dan was gone, our clothes relocated from their various resting points to land at the foot of the bed. There was a soft knock that I realized must have woken me to begin with, and I scooted under the sheet and said "Come in."

194

Dan, freshly showered, brought me my duffle bag. I could hear other voices in the house behind him. I hoped it was just his parents, not the figurines come to life.

"I told them I slept in Eric's room," he said, "And you slept in here."

I nodded. Got out of bed. Unpacked my pajamas, put them on to walk through the hall to the bathroom, showered, returned. Found Dan still sitting on my bed, which was really his bed, which we had made our bed for a few brief moments out of an otherwise eternity.

"Was this okay?" he asked, "Are we okay?" He looked bleary, a little softer around the edges. I sat down beside him and took his hand, held it in my toweled lap, where we watched it for a moment, unsure of what it would do next. I stroked his thumb with my own. I wanted to tell him so much, but the words as usual were lodged like a cough drop between my teeth. I freed his hand and kissed his cheek, and his skin, softer than Doug's and yet harder too, warmed to my touch.

His parents fed us breakfast and small talk, asked no hard questions, made no demands. His mother had a slight accent which I suppose could have been Greek, or could have been learned from the movies. His father was tall and broad and didn't say much at all.   It was obvious they didn't remember me, and I felt strangely fine with that.

Outside the sun was heating quickly and deliriously, drying my still damp hair, burning the all-black truck interior into my bare legs. The little league field was only a few miles away, past the post office and grocery store, across the street from Darling Elementary School, where Doug had met Dan and started this life. I clutched the still unopened package in both hands the whole ride.

When we stepped out of the car there was a slight breeze, a

beautiful lifting feeling that was just like I had hoped. I pulled the red tab on the envelope and inside was a square tin with gold enamel and silver sequins, his name in sloppy cursive inside an ember heart. It looked like a Valentine's Day box a third grader might bring to school. Dan chuckled and I laughed too, and then we were laughing so hard we were crying, or maybe the other way round. We walked to the pitcher's mound, right in the middle of the field, and opened the box together.

"Should we say a few words?" Dan asked, but before I could reply a gust of wind snatched what was left of Doug from between us, and he rose up, up, and up in a glorious cloud.

"I love you," I said to the wind, and my tears burned great tracts of fire down my face. Dan said something I couldn't hear through the roaring on the inside of my ears and I realized we were holding hands like two little kids, tight, fearful, safely crossing.

Dan asked if he could buy me lunch before my flight left, and I couldn't say no. I felt emptied out by the last twenty four hours. I was ravenous. We went to Doug's favorite sandwich place, drank his favorite beer, watched the Cardinals lose horrifically on the television above the counter. Dan paid our bill as I drew patterns in a pile of spilled sugar; a star, a swirl, a heart.

When we said goodbye at the airport I didn't think I'd ever see him again, thought he was gone forever, just like Doug, like the life we would have had together, the family we created, the children we might have made. I put my arms around him and for a moment I just concentrated on keeping my body against his, and his against mine, and breathing in great lungfulls of what might be particles of Doug mixed in with the air all around us.

"If you ever need me," said Dan, "I'm only a phone call away."

"I know," I told him, "ditto."

"Call me when you land," he said, and something broke open inside me, something clicked together. He wouldn't disappear, he was the family Doug and I had made, he was what was left. Even if I never saw him again, I would know he was out there somewhere, scattered among the other people I might meet, or not meet, or marry, or forget. There was a bright line connecting us, holding us together in its strength. And when the plane lifts up, so do my spirits, until I feel I am floating, higher than the clouds, as high as Doug, and I breathe in the plastic filtered air, safe air, contained air, and I sleep.

The Fat Man

I'd been asleep upstairs in my Christmas pajamas, the red ones with the feet that were just a little bit too small and childish but that I still liked to wear, when I was awakened by the sounds of thumping and giggling.

They're meeting Santa without me! I thought nonsensically, and stumbled out of bed, narrowly missing the multicolored metal xylophone I'd been trying to pick out "Silent Night" on before going to sleep. I was very proud of that xylophone, and even more proud that I knew how to spell "xylophone." I'd markered on the letters, one on each key, squishing "ne" together on the smallest note. I snuck down the stairs, still half asleep, and that's when I saw it. My mother, in her best bathrobe, kissing a big bearded man under my father's mistletoe.

At first, I thought it was my father. I had recently begun to suspect that the presents arrived under our tree via Ford Explorer and not reindeer, but had yet to summon enough courage to voice my concerns to anyone else. When I realized that the man my mother was kissing was a full head shorter and twice as fat as my beanpole father, I felt vindicated. *I was right!* I proclaimed inside my head, forgetting that no one had told me otherwise, that my doubts had come from nowhere besides than my own brain. Then I realized that if that man was not my father—who was he? My mother should not be kissing him, that much was clear. She should not be whispering to him, and tickling him, and he should not be touching her arms and back in their silky bathrobe. And neither one of them should be looking at me as I squeaked indignantly on the stairs, peering over the bannister like an orphan waif in a TV holiday special.

"Ezra!" My mother was breathless. "This is—" she lost her momentum, confused. How does one introduce one's lover to one's child, especially if he needs to leave soon in order to make those one night deliveries all over the world?

"Santa Claus." I said, dourly, growing up before their eyes.

"Ezra!" said the bearded man, just as heartily as I'd always imagined, "Funny name for a girl, isn't it?' His chuckle made the one my father did when he read us "The Night Before Christmas" sound pitchy and forlorn.

"I don't know," I said, confused. This was not how Santa was supposed to act. This was not how the mall Santas I had met in the past had acted. They had been friendly but tired and didn't make fun of me.

"It was my grandfather's name," my mother was whispering to him, still holding onto one of this big pink hands. "I was worried we weren't going to have any boys."

This was the first time I had heard this story, and it was far less glamorous than I had hoped.

"Well ho-ho!" said Santa, and his belly moved not so much like a bowl of jelly but more like an overstuffed duffel bag falling down the stairs. "What do you want for Christmas, little girl?"

My mother had a funny expression on her face, like it was trying to smile and hide all at the same time.

"I want a drum set," I said, still perched on the stairs. "With a snare and a foot pedal and also a big gong on the side. And a high hat," I added, not being able to resist showing off that I knew what a high hat was.

"Oh ho!" said Santa again, glancing sideways at my mother, who was definitely frowning and shaking her head.

"We'll see." Santa tapped the side of his nose, a gesture I had often seen my father do which meant absolutely nothing to me. "I can't tell you what's under that tree, now can I? You'll have to wait until morning."

I stared at the colorful boxes next to the fireplace. It looked like a Christmas painting, except that one of the shoulders of my mother's robe had slid down her arm and I could see her lacy bra strap.

"Now go on to bed like a good little girl," Santa adjusted his big black belt buckle.

"Don't you want some cookies?" I asked.

"Oh no no," he laughed a great big chuckle again. "I can rely on your mother to give me something sweet." And he slapped her on the ass, he really did. My mother squeaked just like I had when I saw first saw them, and I ran back to my room as quickly as I could, face burning as bright as his Christmas suit.

Come to find out, my mother's affair had been going on for years, consummated yearly every December and longed for the other three hundred and sixty four days. What we had thought was merely the frenzy of an over enthusiastic lover of holidays was actually a way for her to keep him alive in her mind and libido during the warmer months. No wonder our lights stayed up for months longer than our neighbors, and our glowing Santa Claus statues the most expensive on the block. My mother would spare no expense when it came to her one true love. The Rosenbaums next door would push notes through the mail slot imploring us to take down what they deemed "offensive and insensitive decorations." Our winter electric bills were the talk of the town.

Suddenly, her box of Christmas sweaters was disgusting. I had a crush on Bobby Hendrix who was in the fifth grade, but I wasn't going to wear his face on my chest, now was I? I felt bad for my father, who had always treated my mother's holiday hysteria with good humored charm, only to find out that our Norman Rockwell caroling scene was anything but.

Christmas songs turned pornographic. Hams and turkeys and cinnamon rolls crumbled to dust in our mouths. My brother Daniel, one year younger than me and who probably should have had my name, climbed up onto the roof and threw our heard of reindeer into the street. My mother smiled serenely and informed him that it didn't matter, Santa Claus didn't really use a reindeer driven sleigh anyway, it was just an urban myth.

She moved out by the following Thanksgiving. She and my father tried couples counseling, but she was halfhearted and my father's increasing nervousness as the seasons grew colder only brought the end on faster. When the divorce went through we packed up all her wooden figurines and HO HO HO window decals and burned them in a trash can in the back yard. Mr. and Mrs. Rosenbaum called the fire department, and the police issued my father a warning about bonfires within the city limits.

The wedding was an ornate affair. My mother wore a fur trimmed white gown and a crown that looked like icicles. Janie was a flower girl in a red and white babydoll dress, and Daniel and I wore crushed velvet ensembles the dark green of pine trees. Mine clung to my prepubescent form in all the wrong places, and Daniel developed a rash almost immediately after putting his on. The three of us had elected unanimously to live with our father after the divorce went through, and this was our first visit to "The North," as my mother called her new home.

The ceremony took place in the great room of Claus' mansion. There were crystal chandeliers and a red carpet, just like in Hollywood, and a priest in a bearskin hat who looked very uncomfortable as religion and pop culture mythology merged in front of him. He stumbled through the traditional words, and when she said "I do," my mother looked positively radiant. Janie was picking a scab on her elbow, and Daniel looked itchy and embarrassed. I just felt sad for my father who was back in our Massachusetts suburb watching *MythBusters* and eating takeout without us.

They served reindeer at dinner, which I thought was completely inappropriate but tasted delicious. Daniel and I were each allowed one small glass of champagne in celebration and the bubbles made me sneeze and my head spun all night. We slept in great canopy beds in rooms with personal fireplaces. Janie was scared of the teeth on the bear skin rug and crawled into bed with me. She refused to take off her flower girl dress, and the starchy crinoline scratched me all night long.

At some point after our mother moved out, either my father or Daniel had started calling Claus "The Fat Man," and the nickname stuck. Christmas became a miserable time for us, seeing our families' destroyer plastered happily all over town. We took refuge in the Jewish Community Center but after a while it all felt too fake, like we were missing the point and ignoring everything that had happened to us.

We wandered, lost, for years, trying new hobbies or joining clubs, quitting them all in December and not bothering to rejoin them after New Years. Janie told her middle school friends flatly that our mother was dead and she didn't want to talk about her. She put on black eyeliner and skinny jeans and only wore dark tops and combat boots, but her red and white flower girl dress still hung in the back of her closet, miniature black funeral ribbons pinned all over it. Daniel grew nervous and allergic to everything, breaking out in hives at the slightest sign of velvet or polyester. Our father watched a lot of TV until the wintertime coca cola ads got to him, and he took a new job in Chinatown in Boston where they could be counted on to ignore the holidays completely. I think he liked the hour long train ride each way, staring out the windows and thinking peaceful melancholy thoughts. I saved up my money until I could buy the drum set the fat man had never seen fit to give me. I got a part time job at a local deli, and added to my kit piece by piece, customizing it to my liking and practicing in our garage each night.

Claus was a long distance truck driver on the off months. The long hours and far reaching travel appealed to him, as did the solitude and the noise of the engines. Sometimes my mother would accompany him, and we would get postcards for far away but un-exotic places; "You rock! At the Rock of Ages Granite Mine of Barre VT," "Save the DATE in DAYT-on, OH!" My mother's fondness for kitsch and bad puns may have been what had attracted her to Claus in the first place. He had an endless store of cheeseball humor and outdated jokes that no one under sixty could make sense of without some internet research. The main part of his mansion where the wedding had been was elegant but worn, while his living quarters were replete with lurid and gaudy decorations a cheap antiques dealer would have been thrilled by. It looked like the set of a low budget high school play; tacky lamps sat on pastel davenports, expensive looking plush chairs were reupholstered in polyester and velour; he even had a velvet Elvis painting hung in the master bathroom over the wire basket of oversized shells collected somewhere en route, though through trucking or gift giving he didn't say.

Eventually Daniel and I went off to college and my father remarried, a nice agnostic woman named Barbara who was interested in Tupperware parties and selling junk jewelry on Etsy. She knew, of course, that my father had been married before but I got the feeling she never had all the details. Janie took to her at once and the two could be found camped out at the dining room table, glue-gunning and bedazzling long into the night, Janie's beetle black hair bent next to our step mother's perfectly sprayed and frosted blond updo.

When my dad retired, he and Barb took the traditional route of aging northerners and moved to a condo in Florida. My father had done his research carefully and settled them in the heart of a Jewish community where there was nary a Santa to be seen. When I went to visit them he seemed relaxed for the first time since I was a kid, the sun etching friendly lines into his forehead and deepening his skin to a healthy beige. He had taken up golf and stereotypical Hawaiian shirts, made friends with names like Art and Herman who had wives with thick Brooklyn accents and fingernails the color of their tropical drinks.

My mother, meanwhile, had taken to her new arctic home with such grace that you would never have known she was the same manic woman who had hung icicle lights until three in the morning, tiny children singing carols from the record player inside. She lost weight and color, but in a way that suited her. Janie refused to visit, but Daniel and I did every couple of years and were always greeted by an elegant woman with white streaked hair, one who served us cranberry cocktails and crusty meat pies, left us laden with fur-trimmed gloves and the tacky Christmas sweaters she and Claus warmed themselves with year round.

All the times I visited, I never really felt like I got to know the fat man, partly because my mother most wanted visitors when he was away on his business trips, and partly because I had trouble separating the myth from the man. Claus was pre-diabetic, so he didn't really eat all of those cookies the children left out for him. But who did? He wouldn't say, merely tapped the side of his nose with one finger, the same gesture that had infuriated me as a nine year old. Nearly three decades later I found it insulting as well.

Daniel, who turned out calm and well-adjusted after all, moved to Buffalo and regained complete control over his allergies. He married and had two daughters, both of whom he gave traditional girl's names. He took them to Claus's mansion once, and they ran screaming down the halls, opening doors and slamming them again, watching icicles drip in perfect formation outside of their windows. Claus took them sledding and my mother made them hot chocolate with candy cane stirrers. They braided tinsel in each other's hair and had a far better time than any of us had had as children.

I asked Daniel what he told them when they asked about Claus, but he just shrugged and said "They don't even question. They think it's cool that Santa is one of their grandfathers, and none of their friends believe them. It works out perfectly for everyone."

My father and Barbara sold our old house in Massachusetts to Janie when they left, for an extremely reduced price. She hired some men to paint it emerald green, and soon after moved her internet boyfriend all the way from San Diego to live with her. They adopted five black cats and lived in a perpetual hurricane of feline fur. She cut off all contact with our mother, but flew down once a year to help our father and Barbara with their spring cleaning, which basically consisted of sweeping the dust off Barb's latest craft project outside into the street, where the wind blew it down the block to the Florida sea and the glitter can mingle with the bright white sand.

I live alone in a tiny beach house on the Carolina shore. My closest neighbors are an elderly first generation Mexican couple. At Christmas their large multigenerational family comes to visit, and their porch floods with a pleasant deluge of Spanish and English and baby talk. They play their Latin music as loud as they can, until their neighbor on the other side tells them to turn it down or he'll call the police. It's kind of a Christmas tradition. If I leave my door open while I have my hot chocolate and brandy I can strain my ears and hear the bright wail of the trumpet one of the nephews play, and all of those happy hands clapping along.

Years from now, my father and Barbara will pass on, their condo taken over by another retired couple from the northeast. Janie, Daniel and I will see each other less and less, for Thanksgiving, maybe, a birthday phone call, mailing cards and presents to Daniel's daughters. We will grow old in our separate states, our different colored houses, our pets and spouses and neighbors comforting us in times of need. Eventually we too will die, our bodies returned to the earth, ashes scattered, memorials spoken and erected.

But my mother and Claus will live on, up there in the frozen North, or in storybooks, or memorialized in department store displays each December. They will keep living their strange and self-isolated existence, until the world forgets about them too, and the ice where they make their home slowly embraces them in a final tableau.

Until that day we keep on, facing our strange and interconnected pasts as best we can, both dreading and longing for those first snowflakes of winter and of everything they remind us.

Forever Maze

The boy is too old for this. He pleads for his father to let him go, go to school, go anywhere other than this dusty abandoned building and its company of mice and men. But...

Tony, the father says, *Today you race against Algie.*

Not Algie. Algie is his father's favorite. A big, thick, brown rat, carefully trained, carefully rewarded; a better son than his human son—a smarter son than his human son, smarter even than the mice. Used to be he raced white domestic pet store mice. Then it was brown, dirty ones, caught in his traps in basements and attics, sometimes crawling with lice or other vermin. These were smarter, nastier than the white mice. Now there is Algie. Only Algie.

The prize is not one of cheese or lumps of bread, but of crickets, whose once happy song is cut short by the arrival of this monster killer. Brown fur and black heart. Tony does not like to watch them die, does not enjoy the way their bodies still quiver as Algie bites them in half.

He does not like to watch the way his father does.

The father places Algie tenderly into his maze box, then roughly hands his son another, identical to the first, except there is a sheet of plywood covering the top of this one. A stick is thrust through it. If Tony pushes hard enough on it, it will shift the whole top. He must move the stick through the maze. When it gets to the end, the stick will push through the hole in the bottom. Then Tony will tell his father he is finished, and they can go home.

When Algie reaches the end of the maze, his father will be watching. His father will hold the trained rat lovingly as he runs out the end, into the outstretched palm awaiting him (Algie will not bite his master) and feed him and pet him and return him to his cage.

Tony has pointed out countless times that he has to push an enormous piece of wood with a stick, while all Algie has to do is run.

Of course the rat will be faster.

Of course the rat will win.

But his father only smiles at him, sweet and fake and dangerous, and tells his son not to make excuses; if the rat is smarter and quicker than him, it only proves the theory, the mad reasoning behind all this— that rats are smarter than humans, more quickly conditioned and adaptable.

Today, Tony does not argue. Today, he only wants to get home as quickly as possible. He has seen what his father is building, using pieces of wood where the store has started to fall apart.

It is another maze, of course, it is always another maze. But this is not a tabletop maze, a crude wooden joke. This is a human sized maze, if the human were small enough, crouched over in terror and running forever forward around corners, trying to quell the claustrophobic terror he feels inside—the terror that he will never see daylight aside from the dusty beams that leak in through cracks that have not been smoothly nailed shut. As the walls crush in around him, their rough angular circle shrinking, squeezing, until all he wants to do is stand upright, all he wants to do is feel the glorious unclenching of muscles trying too hard to become smaller, to fit in the tunnel that is the maze. The forever maze. Even as he imagines it, his heart pounds and he has to close his eyes and breathe in slowly until his brain and his blood and his hands go back to normal.

But it is time for today's race.

Tony grabs the outside end of his stick, trying not to wonder what the other end feels like, lost in the dark that way. He hears Algie's desperate chittering and for a moment he can relate to the rat's feral fearful anger. But then it passes, as he hears his father say,

Don't worry Algie, don't worry babe. Just remember what I taught you.

A flash of anger, deep and red, flares in Tony's stomach. His father taught Algie to bite and kill, not just the crickets—but the tame white mice as well.

He remembers his father's laugh of glee when he found his eight prize mice one morning; severed heads in a neat pile under the snarling Algie. And he remembers the times Algie has bitten him—the deep red cuts, which infect and ooze, leaving puckering scars and painful reminders.

He grips the stick harder, determined to win this time. Determined to show his all consuming father which is the smarter son.

Go! his father shouts, and Tony throws all his strength at the stick, shoving the plywood board forward and backward with frustration as the stick hits corner after corner, forcing him to retrace paths he cannot see. He has gotten quite good at mazes over the years, the many, many years, but still worries that his father is right, that Algie is quicker and smarter than he is.

In the background, he can hear his father softly cheering Algie on. In desperation, he shoves the stick too hard, and it starts to crack. He can feel sweat force itself through his skin, under his arms, above his lip, across the wide band of his forehead. He wonders if he might have snagged the stick on the edge of the escape hole. Pulling carefully now, not wanting to damage his instrument of hope any further, he gently wriggles this rod back towards him, and to his great relief it falls into his lap below.

I did it! he shouts, but it is too late—his father holds Algie gently in his hands, and the rat grins mockingly, cradled in the tender hammock of his master's palms.

Wearily, Tony pushes the wooden maze off his knees and stands, stretching the kinks out of his back and legs.

He should have known better than to hope.

He should have known better.

They're heading home now.

Algie, king in his cage, sits between them in the pickup cab. Regally snickering, he throws haughty glances at his master's other son, narcissistically watching his reflection in the rearview mirror as the abandoned supermarket grows smaller and smaller behind him.

Tony is careful to keep his hands in his lap, lest they make any unclean fingerprints on the truck's spotty interior. If he touches so much as a button in the truck, there will be another maze, another two, by himself this time, racing no one but the clock and his father's expectations.

He cannot understand it. The pickup barely stays alive—In cold it shrugs and chortles, coughing as it goes up hills. In heat it gasps and wheezes, heaving sighs as it tumbles down valleys. And yet, none of this is the fault of the machine—another anthropomorphous beast in Tony's life, but is somehow the failing of the boy. One he has learned to ignore.

Or at least to tolerate.

They are home soon. The store is very close to the house, which is of course a ramshackle trailer, squalid with neglect and uncaring, looking like a dumpy, sullen cat pouting in the humid hot. Tony gets out first

211

because the neighbor is there, and his father does not wish to talk to her. He dislikes strangers, so Tony is his distraction. Tony, in an odd, unpleasant way, is proud he can do his father this service, a thing even Algie or the truck cannot.

Hello, says the neighbor. *You're Tony, right?*

He is.

He tries to remember her name, but cannot.

I'm Carrie.

Carrie. She is skinny, almost too skinny, her flesh showing a tender map of the skeleton inside her. He wonders if she has been ill—he has seen that before—or does she starve herself on purpose? He has done that once; when Algie ate the white mice. When he could not bear to touch the meat his father gave him, because in it he saw the pink bloodstained consciousness of eight who had died at the hands of his brother, his father's true son.

Are you all right? It is the neighbor again.

His face must have shown the memory of the white mice. He must learn not to do that—he must make his face a steel plate against which surface his emotions will flatten and spread, unseen except to himself. The way he is sure his father does.

I'm fine. He says, looking out of the corner of his eye. His father and Algie have not yet reached the house, so he must stay and make conversation

How old are you? asks Carrie.

Thirteen, he says, his brain registering the look of surprise which has passed by her metal plate.

He knows he looks younger, and he resents it. If he was bigger, if he was stronger, could he beat Algie at the maze?

Shouldn't you be in school? asks Carrie.

212

I'm helping my father today. he answers the way he has always answered, whenever new neighbors come.

The neighbor nods and goes back to what she was doing—something with plants. Is she trying to grow a garden? Doesn't she know that nothing will grow here?

I keep trying different strains, she says, *But nothing will root properly.*

Then she does know.

It must be drought. She says.

Then again, maybe not.

It's not drought, he says unexpectedly.

She looks at him, curious. He stares uncomfortably back.

Her clothes are stained with earth and growth, while he stinks of sweat and cowardice.

Then he hears the screen door slam, and knows they are inside.

I've got to go. he says.

If she expects him to sound apologetic, then she is disappointed. She is watching the door where is father has gone.

What does your father do? she asks, something in her voice he can't quite read.

He builds things. Tony says. He is very short with her, he has to be. He has to be short with everyone, or they might get behind his struggling metal plate mind and see the terrible creature hidden there.

He moves to go inside.

What kinds of things? she is asking.

He turns briefly for a moment, and they find their eyes locked again, deep and disconcerting.

Mazes, he says. *Always mazes.*

He glances towards the truck where Algie has so recently sat

213

triumphantly.

She follows his eyes, and when she looks back, he is gone; evaporated into the breeze which shuts the screen door.

He immediately goes to his room, a dingy basement space where another child would imagine rats and mice and centipedes creeping through the walls to frighten him. But Tony has no fear of centipedes, and knows that the mice are dead and the rats upstairs where they belong. He sits. Wishes he had a radio, a television, or even a magazine to read. But there is nothing here, only a stained mattress resting on broken bedsprings that squeak in the night.

Today he is thinking about the neighbor, wondering how long she will last before she gives up and leaves this inhospitable town with its unfriendly residents who kill the plants she tries so hard to grow. He finds himself unexpectedly wishing for her flowers to succeed this time.

But then he comes back to his senses, remembers his father, remembers the totalitarian, consuming love he holds over his son's head and the mental torture he can inflict on the boy if he so much as suspects a disloyal thought.

So he forces his mind away from the neighbor, forces his face back into its metal plate shape, and thinks about mazes.

They're eating dinner. Tony watches blankly as his father feeds Algie the best morsels of the slightly raw and gummy meat. He shoves it through the bars of the rat's cage so that it sticks to the metal rods and Algie has to chew it off. He clicks his teeth in pleasure, wishing for more.

Tony stares at the rat as he eats mechanically, one bite, then another, chew chew chew. And the fork goes down, cuts up more, brings it to the mouth, chew chew chew again, as Algie and his father laugh at some hidden joke, probably at his expense.

Suddenly, there is a roar from outside.

His father jumps, dropping Algie's meat on the floor. The rodent protests angrily, but for once his master takes no notice.

What the fuck is she doing? he roars. He is at the window.

Go and stop her, boy. Tony obediently gets up from his place at the table, carefully pushing in his chair.

He opens the front door. Carrie is out there, and she has some sort of noisy machine which is chewing at the earth and making it crumble. The noise has shocked his system and he is slightly frightened for a moment; this is the quietest part of the street. It is a dead end, so no cars pass by except their own, and it goes only to the broken Shop n' Save where the road stops.

He steps outside.

Excuse me, he says, the image of politeness, *Do you think you could stop that? My father and I are having dinner.* but she doesn't hear him over the noise.

Steeling himself, he walks up to her and taps her shoulder. She takes what look like globs of putty from her ears.

Excuse me, he says again, *Do you think you could stop that? My father and I are having dinner.*

Of course, she says, *I'm sorry. When would be a better time to do it?*

He thinks for a moment. He wants to tell her: not at all. My father and Algie do not like the noise.

He wants to tell her: all night long. My father and Algie do not like the noise.

215

But instead he says,

How about tomorrow, after we leave.

Where do you go?" she asks, *I've seen you leave every day at eleven o'clock sharp. What is it you do?"* she asks, merely curious. But it is an invasion of privacy.

I will not tell her! His brain thinks, but his mouth is too far ahead of him.

To the store. it says, *My father builds things.*

She nods, and turns off her machine.

Inside, his father growls at him.

What took so long?

She couldn't hear me, he explains, *Over the noise of the engine.*

His father growls again, wordless this time, and Tony tries to make himself disappear.

Algie ate your dinner, his father says.

Tony stares at his chipped plastic plate, where the rat sits amid scraps of food. He cannot imagine how Algie could eat so much. Surely he will become huge, grotesque. He has a fleeting moment of hope— perhaps the forever maze is not made for him, perhaps it is made for an overly large Algie, grown two foot or three, scrambling amid the planks, grubby fur leaving dirt smudges to mark his path.

But then his father laughs, a huge laugh, one used only for Algie, and Tony remembers who the maze is for.

The next day, they return again to Shop n' Save, as they always do, at eleven o'clock sharp. Tony thinks he hears Carrie starting up her machine as they leave the driveway. He is nervous today—the forever maze is boring a hole in his head.

216

But it is not today.

Today it is another race with Algie.

Another loss.

Another triumphant ride home for the father and the rat-son.

Another monotonous gloomy homecoming, broken only by the sight of Carrie planting next door.

Hello, she says warmly, as his father takes Algie and goes inside.

Hello, he says, not wanting to seem to cold, but not eager to talk, either.

I'm planting tomatoes, she says.

He does not have the energy to tell her it is useless, that the fabric strips she uses to tie the tiny plants to stakes may as well be nooses.

He hears the screen door slam, and goes inside.

It stays the same for a week.

Then one day, his father leaves him behind. He leaves at eleven o'clock sharp without Tony, without Algie. Tony's internal clock tells him it is time to go, but there is no father. There is no pickup. And Carrie has started her machine.

Algie, in his cage, is screaming angrily. Tony does not go near him. His fingers remember being bitten and stabbed by cactus spine teeth and needle claws. Instead, he goes outside.

Carrie sees him immediately. He's not sure he wanted her to, but there she is.

Why aren't you with your father? she asks him. Questions, it is always questions with this neighbor.

He's building on his own today. he says.

What does he build again? she asks.

Mazes.

217

He's said it. Again. He didn't mean to tell her. He turns quickly and hurries back inside.

Wait! Carrie calls after him. He stops and turns, remembering just in time to put his feelings behind the metal plate.

Are you all right? she asks him.

He nods. What else is he to do?

Okay, she says. *Tony...* he stops his flight once more. *If you ever want to talk—I'm here. You can talk to me.*

He nods curtly.

I don't, he says, *I can talk to my father.*

"Okay," she again, but she doesn't believe him, he can tell. He doesn't even believe himself.

As he turns away this time, he sees her put the putty back in her ears. If he had putty like that, he wonders, could he stop up the cracks in the steel plate? Stop the thoughts from leaking out?

He half turns to ask her where she got it, but she is still watching him, one hand on her ear. He turns quickly around and goes back inside.

He intends to, anyway. But then he remembers that Algie is waiting for him, Algie is screaming and crying like the brother he never had, the brother he would have so much rather had. So he turns to the side of the house instead, to where the lattice work once lined the bottom of the porch stops.

When he was younger, he could crawl inside and hide there. Hide from whatever make-believe monsters and chimeras haunted him. When his mind aged, and his body grew larger, it was harder to fit, and the monsters were no longer make-believe. Now, at thirteen, he is small for his age, but it is still tight. And he remembers the claustrophobia of the Forever Maze and is not sure that he wants to go under there at all.

But he thinks of Algie again, and decides this is a better way.

Anything is a better way.

He crawls forward, pulling himself with elbows and knees. He crawls forward until he can see Carrie and her machine. He watches for a long time, until his muscles begin to stiffen, and he begins to long to change positions, to ease the aches, just like he was afraid he would. And the space under the porch begins to grow smaller as he watches the neighbor and her machine.

Then suddenly, she stops, and does a strange thing.

She steps over the fence. She steps over the fence, into his father's yard. She steps over the fence and walks towards the house.

What is she doing? Is she going to go inside? Will she walk on the porch over his head? Will she be caught, another piece added to his father's endless puzzle of experimentation?

He cannot help himself, he crawls out of his space as quickly as possible.

Stop! He cries out as loud as he can, louder than he has ever shouted before in his life. He can feel the steel plate fall away from his face, but he doesn't care, he must stop her, he *must* stop her—can't she see what she's doing, can't she see what will happen to her? His internal clock is telling him his father is due home any second, and he doesn't want him to find her here, doesn't want the same thing that happened to his mother to happen to her, doesn't want his father to have any reason to yell at him tonight, but most of all, *he does not want him to put her in a maze.*

Stop! He shouts out again, his skinny legs thrusting at the ground again and again, pushing it away from him, pushing his body towards her.

Stop! Is he crying? He thinks he might be; he thinks he might feel

219

tears on his face, but when he reaches up to see, there is nothing there, nothing except a dead leaf hanging from his hair.

Stop! It is the last time he will say it, he can feel his unused voice giving out; already his throat is parched and clawing at itself, trying to find a drop of water.

But is has worked, she has stopped her hypnotic parade of one. She is standing still, watching him come towards her. If she thinks he will stop, if she thinks he will ever stop until his legs give out, she is wrong. As he runs by, he grabs her arm, the one which holds the machine, and pulls her along beside him, until they reach the fence.

Then he stops.

Go, he wheezes, grabbing at his throat.

Go and don't come back. You can't come back. He won't like it. My father—my father doesn't like people poking around. He doesn't like strangers—only rats. She's staring at him again.

She climbs back over the fence.

Let me help you. she pleads.

I don't need any help. He tries to put the steel plate back onto his face, but he doesn't think it's working. He couldn't be sure. Not unless he had a mirror.

Just don't come back. He turns to leave, but she grabs his hand and squeezes it.

Please, Tony. She looks into his eyes. He can only stare at her a second before it makes him uncomfortable. He has to struggle to keep the remains of the plate over his eyes and mouth. He shakes his head, afraid. So she lets him go. What choice does she have?

But as he turns to go, he sees something.

One of her tomatoes has a new leaf.

220

His feet drag as he goes inside. They want to become part of the dirt which they so recently flung away, but he rejects this idea with horrified revulsion. He cannot breathe through his exhausted throat. For once, he cannot hear Algie's rude demands. For once, thoughts of himself begin to crowd out the other's suggestions.

All he can think about is water. He finds his cup, chipped and plastic to match the plate, and fills it from the tap. The water is sweet and metallic, bloodlike, but it is beautiful. He has another cup, and another.

What did she mean, help him? What could she do?

When his father comes home, he is in a good mood. But then Algie tells him about the day. About the way Tony didn't feed him at all. About the way Tony didn't give him any water.

About the way his father wasn't there.

Then his father gets upset. He starts to glare at Tony, who has not moved from the table where he sat drinking water. He takes Algie out of his cage and strokes him. He pets his brown rat-fur too hard, and Algie screams at him. For the first time ever, Algie is ornery with his master.

The man roars, and flings Algie back into his cage.

See what you did! he shouts at Tony, *"Even Algie has turned against me! First your mother, then you, and now Algie! My prize, my joy, my baby—what have you done? What are you doing? Where have you been all day? The only day I leave you at home—just one day I want to be by myself, and you cannot even feed him. It's not much I ask of you—just a little help, a little help and I let you live here, I give you food and clothes and a place to live and a noble cause to work for, and I can't even leave you alone for one day! You worthless piece of shit!*

he raises his hand and hits Tony across the face. He puts his whole arm into it, his whole body it seems, his whole soul, if there is one left in the mad, distorted frame. Tony, with barely a moan, falls off his chair onto the floor, where he curls into a ball, etching fear in every tightening muscle, every straining bone. His father looks at him and snarls.

But Tony thinks he sees fear in his father's eyes also. Just a touch; perhaps his own steel plate is not hinged as tightly as Tony thought.

His father has never hit him before.

Has never hit him, has never even touched him. He must have, when Tony was very small, but he can't ever remember feeling his father's hand before. It has shocked him so severely that he is unable to move, would be unable to defend himself had his father's arm struck again.

Luckily, it does not.

Day after tomorrow, the father hisses, *Day after tomorrow we're all going to the store. I have a surprise for you, boy.* He picks up Algie's cage, and walks out.

A surprise. It won't be a surprise, will it? It will be a giant maze of broken planks and broken dreams. A forever maze.

Lying there, mind pulsating in time with the throbbing of his cheekbone where his father has struck him, Tony makes up his mind.

The next day, he sleeps late. He has not done so in a very long time, and it feels glorious. When he at last rises from his mattress, his legs are stiff and aching. His calves protest as he climbs the stairs into the kitchen.

Algie is there in his cage again, and wakes when he sees the boy enter. He shouts that he is thirsty, and Tony fills a cup with water and pours it through the bars of the cage into the rodent's dish. Algie turns around, surprised at this rare bit of attention, but decides to drink the water anyway. What stories will he tell his master now, Tony wonders?

There is no breakfast, there never is. There is no food unless his father is there. So he drinks a glass of water and goes outside.

The sun is high, but Carrie does not have her machine today. Instead, she is kneeling by her tomato plants.

He walks over to see.

What are you doing? he asks.

I'm pulling them out, she explains. *They're all dead—all but these two.* She points to the one Tony has seen the day before, and another that grows next to it. Both sport new leaves.

You're not with your father today? she is making conversation again, and he wishes she wouldn't.

No, he says.

There is silence between them.

In the distance he can hear Algie's chitterings. He thinks he hears the truck coming back.

Tomorrow, after we leave, dig up the floor of my bedroom, he says.

It wasn't the truck, it wasn't anything at all. His father doesn't come home until late that night. It must have taken him a long time to finish the forever maze.

When he comes home, he is tired. Too tired to give Tony his dinner. Too tired, even, to give Algie his dinner. So they go to bed without eating. Tony hasn't eaten since yesterday, and it makes him feel a little lightheaded. But soon he falls asleep and it doesn't matter anymore.

In the blackness of very early morning, he awakes out of a nightmare

223

that he can't remember. It was something about a maze, he's sure of it. Another claustrophobic crawlspace, worse than the space under the porch, because he could always go backwards there, he knew how to get out of it. But in the forever maze there is no going backwards. There is only one exit, only one entrance. One cannot be substituted for the other.

He curls up on the mattress, touching his bruising cheek, and thinks about tomorrow. Thinks about the forever maze. There is a kind of blank terror hiding behind his steel plate. He knows Algie will beat him again, knows it as he knows the inevitability of death. But why does the rat always win?

He feels as though he is missing some key piece of information. Why should a rat beat a human? Humans are larger, faster, smarter. Maybe rats are just luckier.

It is morning. It is eleven o'clock sharp. They are in the pickup, heading for the store. Tony cannot hear Carrie's machine.

He woke up earlier than usual today. He wanted to give himself time to prepare, hours to practice sealing the cracks in the plate over his emotions. He thinks he has been successful. He thinks that, after today, no one will ever know what he thinks again.

They are at the store. They are here. Here is the maze.

It's not hidden anymore, but looming menacingly in front of the store, where they always race. Where they will always race.

That's it son, says his father, *that's today's maze.*

Son. His father has never called him that. Tony wonders, was he talking to him or to Algie?

They get out of the pickup and walk over to the maze.

His father's hand caresses the splintery planks.

224

Algie has his own maze, up on the top. So that way, you can't cheat and follow him.

His father laughs uproariously to the sky. Tony feels vaguely ashamed at his stupidity. He hadn't even thought of that.

Maybe rats are smarter, he thinks now. *Maybe they do deserve to win.*

Are you ready? his father asks.

No—the word has somehow slipped out from behind the steel plate. What will his father do now? Will he hit him again? Will he smile knowingly at Algie?

Instead, he laughs. He is jovial today.

Of course you're ready. You're always ready for another maze! Although he does not say it, Tony knows that this is the last maze. Oh, there will be others, little lap-top mazes as before, but this is the big one. This will tell which son is worthy of the father's affection. And with a dread heavy in his chest, Tony knows it will be Algie.

Here you are. His father opens a little door on one side. Tony has to crouch down to go through it. He can hear his father shut the door, and there is a clunk as another board is put over it. Then there is the pounding of a hammer. His father is nailing the door shut!

No—says Tony again, it seems to be the only word he knows.

Don't shut it, please—he wants to scream. He wants to cry his rage and fright out to the world, but he knows there is no one listening.

He can hear his father's muffled voice.

I'm putting Algie in next. When you hear me say go, you run for the end. You can run now boy, eh? No more excuses about a stick—now you and Algie are equal! But that's what worries Tony the most. That he and Algie may not be equal after all. That the rat may be the better of the two.

225

He hears noises above him, a scrabbling, and then his father nails Algie's door shut too.

Go! he hears, but he cannot move.

It it just like his nightmare.

Only worse.

It is everything he feared, only more so, because now he's here, now the maze is not just in his mind anymore.

The tunnel is short, and narrower than he expected. His is bent over at the waist, and still his head touches the ceiling, so he bends his knees too. He has to make his shoulders go diagonally so he doesn't get stuck in the tunnel. He has to try to make his mind go blank so he doesn't get stuck in his fear.

He is sweating already. He is sweating like a pig, only he has heard somewhere that pigs don't actually sweat. Why is he thinking about pigs at a time like this? He should be thinking about rats. About how rats think. About how Algie thinks so cleverly that he can beat him every time.

He forces his right foot forward. He tries to move the left foot, but cannot. It is too dark. If only there were a little light—if only he could see just a little—

But wait. There is a little light, if he can just walk forward three or four steps. Just a little bit ahead.

I can do it, he tells himself, *I can beat Algie.* He sees the light. He touches it. It is just as he predicted when he first saw the forever maze—there is a space in the wall where the boards do not quite meet. He can put four of his fingers up to the bigger knuckle through the space. His fingers are free—they are outdoors.

How does it feel, fingers? he whispers. *What does the outside feel like?* He moves them slightly. He imagines a breeze. He pulls them

226

back through and sinks down onto the pavement beneath him. He cannot go on. He cannot. Algie has won.

He sits there for a long time. Long enough so that his eyes adjust to the dark, to the meager light spilling in from the disconsolate cracks. Long enough so that the hard asphalt floor and creaking wooden walls seem to close in on him, squish him down so that he has no room for himself, so that soon all the life will be crushed out of him, and there will be only his spirit, trapped in this little artificial box.

His breathing starts to quicken. This is not the way he wants to die! It should not have to be like this—he should be free.

He tries to stand, but his legs are shaking so much they cannot hold him up. Breathing so hard and so quick that he is panting, he pulls himself along the floor. He has to get out. He has to be free, to get out of this box, out of the blind panic which is the Forever Maze. But somewhere inside him, he knows that his father has not put an exit on this maze. There is no way out, there is only forward and backward for all eternity.

For Forever.

He comes to his first crossroads. Left or right, which should he choose? Left. He crawls on, agonizingly slowly, ripping his jeans where they drag along the pavement.

Another crossroads. Left or straight on? He chooses left again.

A little bit farther, only a little bit farther, he sings it to himself, and it becomes his whole being, a rhythm to crawl to, a reason to crawl, a prayer.

A little bit farther along is a wall. It is a dead end.

No, his whispers, quiet as a mouse, quiet as a rat. What now? What does he do?

He is frightened beyond any imaginings, beyond any time he has

227

been frightened before. There is nothing worse than this dark, claustrophobic hole. Nothing.

He turns around, and is immediately disoriented. Which way to turn? There are too many options. He closes his eyes, but that makes it worse. Eyes closed, there is no light at all, and his mind is free to conjure up nightmare figures of three foot long Algies, muscular and evil, running through the maze ahead of him, always ahead of him.

He crawls a little bit farther. And a little bit farther. His arms are starting to weaken, but he pushes on, around corners, back and forth, backwards and forwards, completely disoriented and lost. Is he at the center of the maze? A corner? Or some forgotten extremity that leads to nowhere?

He does not know, does not think he will ever know.

At last his arms can hold him no longer, and he struggles to his knees. There is a dull pain; perhaps they are scraped or even cut completely open, letting his blood flow into the manmade earth beneath him.

He pushes on, always a little bit farther, a little bit farther.

When he reaches the next wall, he collapses, still panting, his mouth so dry he can no longer feel his tongue and lips. For a brief moment, his need for water overrides his claustrophobia. He imagines his chipped plastic cup. He imagines a fountain, he imagines a well. Out in the sunlight—the sunlight! He realizes the light through the cracks is not as bright as it has been. It must be late afternoon, it must be nearly evening, and then nearly night. No! He cannot let himself be in the maze when night comes! When night comes it will be pitch black, and even the moon and stars will not be bright enough to flow through the cracks and show him the way out.

Panicked again, unable to see or think or feel, he lets out a wordless

228

howl, loud and long an inhuman.

And then he hears his father's truck.

He is leaving! Has Algie won then—or is his father glad to be free, glad to finally be rid of all his burdens?

Tony shouts again in rage and fear—and then is suddenly quiet.

The missing piece falls into place, it is a revelation of his own.

He knows how to beat Algie.

It is not by skill or luck or speed.

It is by brains.

It is by intelligence.

He knows how to get out of here, he knows how to beat the maze that may or may not have an exit.

He puts his hands above his head, palms turned upwards, and stands up suddenly, forcing his body upward, through the roof.

It yields, then creaks apart, and Tony's head and torso shoot through.

There is more pain than he has ever known—he feels blood on him, but he cannot feel where it is coming from. Perhaps this is the end, perhaps he will die now. He feels a certain peace. At least it will not be in a wood and asphalt box.

Then a shape comes out of the darkness and hurls itself at his chest. It is a nightmare pack of Algies three feet long, attracted by the scent of blood on the boy. The largest one is on top of him, ripping at his chest, trying to get to his heart.

Shrieking and screaming, Tony realizes he has broken through to Algie's maze box. He paws at the thing on his chest, trying to be rid of it, not even feeling the pain it inflicts on his body, only on his mind.

With his new strength of human revelation, he breaks off the ceiling of the second box, and finds he is on the outer wall of the maze.

He grabs hold of the thing on his chest, and flings it hard onto the ground.

It stops moving. It is only Algie, little Algie, still and quiet in death. He feels his throat swelling up, feels it twist and knot inside him.

And then he notices the cars.

There are three of them; his father's truck, a blue police car, and a white car that he does not recognize.

Then Carrie gets out of the white car, and he thinks he must be dreaming. Skinny Carrie from next door is here. To help him. He hopes, he prays, it is to help him.

Then she is running towards him, and he climbs over the wall of the maze in a dream.

The woman in the basement, she says, *In the wooden box, is she your mother?*

He nods, tries to whisper through his strangled throat.

He didn't killed her. Carrie is telling him. She puts her hands on his shoulders, she almost shakes him. *Do you hear me Tony? He didn't kill her. It's all right. He didn't kill her. He buried her there, but he didn't end her life.*

Tony feels his metal plate melting. It is melting all down his face, mixing with the blood on his knees, on his hands, on his chest. It melts away, and he realizes he will never see it again.

Carrie puts her arms around him, and he clings to her like a tiny child, weeping as he has never done before.

In the background, he hears his father laughing.

Moonfriend

When they are young, they play together under the moonlight. She calls him her *moonfriend*. Cyrus, dear Cyrus, is different from the other children, but then, so is she. His parents give him what he needs and leave him alone, while her mother pays her the wrong kind of attention. The more she is home, the worse the beatings become, so she escapes out the window of her cellar bedroom to climb the trellis on the house next door. His house. And he gives her old jackets and sweatshirts to cover the worn, too small undershirts and torn jeans that are all she has.

In his house, or under the moonlight, she is warm and protected. But once she goes home, the nightmare begins.

In fourth grade he moves away and the beatings, miraculously, cease. He doesn't say goodbye, he doesn't call or write. She accepts this as she has accepted everything else the adults in her life have thrown at her, but she misses him. There is no one to ask questions to, and no one to explain. Sometimes she stares at his house for hours, wondering where he went and what he is doing now. She makes up stories in her head, fairy tales full of magic and traveling and happy endings, stories where everything is full of explanations and wrapped up neatly. In real life his old house lies dormant and sleeping, the For Sale sign growing ivy and swaying in the dusty wind. No one will buy it.

Marie makes the sign of the evil eye every time she passes. She spits twice in fast succession, one on each side of the sign. Juny doesn't know if she is trying to prevent Cyrus' family from coming back, or if she doesn't want the house to sell at all. Marie likes her privacy. She has things to hide.

At first, Juny leaves her window open every night, ready for a quick escape if she needs one. In her dreams she flies out the window like a bird, or a bat, and into the house next door where Cyrus has been waiting for her all this time. She will blow the dust off of him as he sleeps and then they will rise together, hand in hand, all the way up to the moon.

Months go by, and then years, and Marie, if not exactly kind, makes sure the cupboards are stocked with food and occasionally leaves a wad of damp and crumpled bills on her daughter's bed for clothes and other necessities. The tight wrinkles around her mouth and eyes loosen, and her menacingly large figure relaxes into soft dough. She pours her bottles full of heavy colored liquids down the drain, douses herself in rosaries and flowery perfume.

Juny still shivers in the cold, but repairs the cellar window she no longer needs to climb through. She makes new friends; other little girls from school with clean hair and gentle parents. Despite her life at home, she isn't excluded. Somehow she manages to hold onto that charisma and open honesty the other children so admire.

Life isn't good, but it's livable.

Then he comes back.

She hasn't seen him for eight years, but when a figure moves across the window next door she knows at once who it is. She can barely contain her joy. She runs upstairs, and finds Marie at the table, a glass dwarfed in her meaty hand, a bottle by her elbow. She stops. She hasn't seen Marie drink since before Cyrus moved away, so many years ago.

"What?" Marie growls. There is a loud, dull smell filling the air, overpowering the normally rosy scent of Marie's skin. It is dirt and moss and mold, and something darker, something decaying and sour.

"I—" she doesn't want to say it, but the words burst out. "Cyrus is back."

Marie sweeps the bottle off the table where it smashes on the floor, and crushes the little glass in her hand. Flecks of blood appear on her palm, staining the blotchy skin.

"You are not to see him Juny, do you hear?" Marie's voice is icy cold, but rises to a shout. "You are not to see him!"

Juny backs off, terrified. This is the Marie who vanished eight years ago, when the neighbors left.

She turns to go downstairs, but in two quick strides Marie is upon her, pinching and slapping. She curls up into a ball, shielding her face with her hands, but Marie is so much bigger. Juny's bony wrists tenderize the meat of her blows. She opens her eyes and catches sight of the old Marie again, the pinched mouth, the eyebrows drawn close together on her forehead, and something else, something Juny hadn't been able to recognize as a child. She sees fear light up the corners of Marie's eyes, sees it make her nostrils flare open and her purple tongue flick out in concentration. Marie bites her lower lip, hard, and takes aim.

When the pain grows and darkness threatens the edges of her vision, Juny tumbles halfway down the stairs, and catches herself on the banister. She eases downward, checking to see that she can still walk. Bruised but not broken she thrusts an arm though the patched up window, barely even feeling as the jagged glass cuts her skin. She's bigger than she used to be, and almost doesn't fit, but manages to pull herself through and run next door.

The trellis is a little rotten but she makes it up, hoping and praying that he will be there. And he is, almost as if he knew she was coming. He watches her climb through the window.

233

"I'll get the ice," he says, and is back a moment later with a bowl of cold relief and a roll of bandages.

"Did she do this to you?" He asks, as he examines the ugly scratches on her arm.

She is trembling and weeping, the tears running down her cheeks in the room she hasn't cried in since she was seven years old.

"The window—" she tries to speak. "I climbed through the window—" She takes a breath, steadying herself. He doesn't say anything, but she can imagine what he sees. The same skinny, helpless girl with the scraggly blond pigtails he left behind eight years ago. For a moment, time has stopped, and it's as if nothing has ever changed. Then he speaks again, and the spell is broken. She may be the same scared child, but he has grown. His voice has lowered and softened, his eyes deepened and his hair lengthened. His body has stretched and changed in a way she feels certain hers has not.

"Who bandaged you while I was gone?" he asks.

"No one." She shakes her head, but stops; the movement makes her nauseous.

"She didn't touch me til I told her you were back." He flinches, so slightly that for a moment she's not sure she saw him move. But when she looks into his eyes, she knows what she saw, and what's more, she thinks she knows what Marie saw.

"Can you help me?" She whispers, barely even making a sound in the suddenly quiet room. A cricket throbs in the growing darkness.

He sighs and stands, throwing his glance around the room as if searching for something.

"Here." He takes a little brass nob with a gold chain strung through it off of its' resting place on the window lock. He hands it to her, and

234

she takes it hesitantly, as if expecting it to come alive in her hand. She looks at him, unable to voice all questions the night has raised.

"Put it on," he says. When she doesn't move, he takes it back and slips it over her head. The nob's slight weight hangs down between her breasts, strangely comforting in its metallic chill.

Her thin white shirt is ripped down the side, stained with dirt and blood. He helps her take it off, and gives her an old gray sweatshirt. Then he gives her a hug, something she's sure he's never done before, and helps her to the bed. She lies down carefully, drawing the blankets up around her.

"Cyrus—" she starts, but he shakes his head. She watches him pull the chair up next to the window. The moonlight shines on him and makes his face a mass of shadows. She clasps the brass nob in her hand and closes her eyes. Just before she falls asleep she thinks she feels it pulse, just once.

When she awakes in the morning, he is standing in front of the window, blocking the sun in a Cyrus-shaped cloud.

"Get up." He says. He doesn't turn around.

She finds the pain has diminished, and so she does. The brass nob has made an imprint in her hand. She is reminded briefly of the drops of blood spotting Marie's palm.

"What time is it?" She joins him at the window.

"Early."

"Will I see you again?" She's not sure why she asks. Whenever she needed him before, he has been there.

He turns to look at her, but doesn't answer. She squeezes his hand, and climbs out the window.

Halfway down, the rotted wood on the trellis breaks, and she falls the rest of the way. She is unhurt, and gets up and runs easily across the lawn, stopping once to look back at his house.

She crouches down by her basement window, but abruptly stands up again, an unexpected thought invading her. Why not? Taking courage, she walks around the house to the front entrance. She stuffs the brass nob and chain beneath Cyrus' sweatshirt, and opens the door.

The hallway smells faintly of alcohol, with the reek of rotten flowers hovering beneath it. Entering the kitchen, she finds Marie at the table, ringed by a semicircle of empty bottles.

"Where have you been?" Marie starts to stand, but grabs the back of the chair and unsteadily sits again.

"Asleep," Juny answers.

"No you haven't." Marie sways slightly. "I went down there and checked."

"You never check."

"I did tonight."

They stare at each other in the empty silence. Is Marie still frightened? She cannot tell through the haze of booze and hate.

"I was at Cyrus'" Juny says finally. Finding new strength, Marie stands abruptly and cuffs her daughter across the ear. Juny stumbles, shaking her head, but realizes the blow didn't hurt.

Marie hits her again and again, but nothing happens. Not so much as a scratch marks her skin. She lifts the nob from under her shirt and stares at it in wonder.

Suddenly, it is snatched away, a huge hand breaking the thin chain it hangs from.

"Did that—that witch give this to you?" Marie dangles the charm between them. She sneers like a jack o' lantern, yesterday's makeup blurring her features together.

"Give it back!" Juny grabs at it desperately, but Marie pulls it away. In one quick movement, she slides the nob off the broken chain and swallows it.

Juny cries out as Marie comes towards her. But it still doesn't hurt. Marie stands back, confused, shaking her head like a dog. She opens and closes her injured hand and says something so fuzzily that Juny can't make out.

Gathering the shards of her broken courage around her once more, Juny walks past Marie, back down the hallway, and out the door. Marie looks up only once, then shakes her head again as if trying to clear it. She keeps clenching and unclenching that one hand, watching it as if something will change.

Outside, Juny debates which way to go. She briefly considers returning the sweatshirt to Cyrus, but she knows that better things await her in the opposite direction. He'll understand.

He always does.

The Path of Bones

It starts out as a maze of footprints, cat sized at first, growing larger and larger the longer you follow it. There are innumerable twists and turns. The path is mostly through forest and you almost lose it many times among the dense underbrush. You wonder how many days you had wasted scrabbling through the thorns and brambles, and if maybe it would have been easier to follow the main road.

When you reach the town you stay in an inn. No one bothers you. You have sticks in your hair and your arms are ripped and bleeding. They think you are a wild thing, perhaps an animal adding to the footprints of the path. Perhaps they are right.

On the other side of town the path changes. You have trouble finding it at first, as you were expecting footprints so deep you had to climb in and out of them. Instead, it is hides tamped down and sewn together, staked into dirt and ground into rocks. You name them as you walk along; one step for snake, two for hare, three for coyote, five for bear. The furs are gentle and you take your boots off. The varying thicknesses of the pelts are a welcome change from the unending stiffness of the inside of your boots. After a while the fur became worn down and you can feel the rocks beneath it. Ancient hairs sharp as spines prick your soles. You put your boots back on.

A vast gray expanse of elephantine leather lays in front of you. It is a river of deceased herbivore. Powdery decay fluffs up around you with every step. It gets in your eyes, your hair—it clogs your lungs until you cough and cough. Your canteen has long since dried up. You hope the next town is close. You miss the forest. The land beyond the path has turned to sand as far as you can see, which isn't very far due to all the dust.

At one point the path disappears. Years of walkers have destroyed the tapestry, and desert winds have blown the remnants away. You plod on in what you hope is the right direction, and eventually come to a walkway of jewels.

It is beetles, you realize on closer inspection, beetle carapaces turned to fossil in the sun. They glimmer green and blue and gold, and you glide along them smooth as ice. When night falls they wink like stars, and you find a renewed vigor in your bones. You feel you could walk all night, but eventually you tire and set up camp to one side of the path where you can watch it as you fall asleep. You have never seen another traveler and have long ceased to worry about theft or abduction.

In the morning the beetle path is just as inviting, and you pack up quickly, eager to get back on it. There is still no water, but you feel hopeful about things to come.

As the day wears on, the beetle backs dull and the greens become browns and the blues fade away. By mid-afternoon your feet crunch with every step as once-hard shells break around you. The path becomes rockier, the desert disappears. Everywhere is ugly and barren. Tiny trees spit up out of what looks like sheer rock. They point spindly fingers at you and shower the path with dried out husks. You're not sure what the path is made of now, some sort of bug, perhaps one with hairy legs and millions of eyes. It is disturbingly soft.

The dark comes fast and suddenly around the rising cliffs, and you set up camp directly on the path, afraid to stray too far and fall into a crevasse. You are tired but you cannot sleep. The wind howls and sings too loudly and you keep thinking you feel the ground move beneath your tent. It is your second full day without water.

The morning is still, and when the path begins to change again you know you are nearing the end of your journey. Mixed in with the remains of the spiders and centipedes is something white and chalky, a smooth powder which becomes rougher and sharper the further you go, splintering and crackling beneath your feet like tiny impersonal twigs.

It is the stuff of legends. As the path continues you find yourself spit out of the mountains and into a pine forest, tree trunks ancient and primeval and thicker than two of you, yellow needles slicing down with a sound like soft rain. A gentle breeze blows through the treetops, tiny above you.

Soon the path's edges are ringed with a primitive fence of bones, they grow larger and larger until each one is bigger than you are. You try to imagine what they could be; whale, mammoth, dinosaur? You are so tiny compared to all that surrounds you. You are an insignificant speck of sand, one of countless others who went before you. You have never felt so important.

You stick to the middle of the path, where endless feet have worn the bone to filmy dust. When you stop to rest, you have to climb over the fence to find somewhere to sit that is not sharp. The pine floor is a relief, and you take off your boots to stretch your feet. Little teeth sprinkled on the trail have imbedded themselves into your soles, and you must pluck them one by one, careful to return them to the path when you resume your journey.

The air begins to change and the breeze grows stronger. There is a tangy scent, and it soothes your parched throat and chapped lips. It reminds you of something, something from long ago. It is a comforting smell, and it wraps you in its aroma like armor and you find you can run.

Your feet stop hurting, and you no longer feeling the ancient fingers and toes that seek to claw through the soles of your boots. You seem to fly now, along the endless rows of trees and the bleached white parchment of the path. Up ahead there is a break in the monotony, and when you soar out between the trees you see it: the ocean, vast and gray and sparkling before you.

There is no bird call. There is nothing but the gentle shush of the waves against the shore, a dusk yellow stretch that crawls on as far as you can see. You slow your pace, wanting to savor the freshness of this place, the peace and tranquility of your final destination.

The path has turned to sand as well, and your feet sink in gratefully with each step. As you climb the rise among the razor sharp dune grass you see a little cabin to your left. It sits right on the edge of the water, one end spinning out on stilts, languishing in a sunny porch. There is a figure at the end, who waves. You raise your hand to her, and she runs through the door. You know what she has gone to do, who she has gone to tell. Inside that cabin everyone is waiting, and they will all be very glad to see you.

You hurry now, again, although you know you have all the time in the world.

Publications and Permissions

www.ingramcontent.com/pod-product-compliance
Lightning Source LLC
Chambersburg PA
CBHW060916250626
47159CB00008B/3027